The Final Assassin

Rev. Ronald E. Fraker

DEDICATION

I would like to dedicate this book to my wife Sandy and my entire family, along with the many friends and supporters who have encouraged me as I have traveled this long road called life. Without God, family, and friends, we are truly alone. God bless each one, and may the peace of God lead you in everything you do.

CONTENTS

ACKNOWLEDGMENTS

I would like to thank those who have read this book and made great suggestions and given Godly advice concerning this manuscript. Those people are: Sandy Fraker, Brenda Fraker, Elvin and Janet Wood, and Tara Buckwald. Thank you to each one.

I would like to thank Dr. Victor Ehiemere and the staff at Palette Ink for their excellent work on the cover design and Rhema Ehiemere who assisted with this manuscript and preparation for publication. Both men are anointed authors, and their talents and spiritual insights have made it possible for this book to be published.

CHAPTER ONE
IN PRISON
INTRODUCTION

I was tired!

I was cold!

I was hungry, and I was in the foulest mood I had been in for a long time.

You asked, "Why are you in this foul mood?

I told you why I was in this foul mood. I was seventy-three years old, and I had been sitting in that stinky, dank jail cell for about three months. To pile misery on top of my misery, the guards had crammed about one hundred other prisoners into that same jail cell.

Every morning the guards congregated outside of one of the ten jail cells and loudly called out four or five names. They repeated this procedure for each cell. When they called the prisoners' names, the prisoners were expected to walk to the cell door for their scheduled executions. This daily routine had been very peaceful as each prisoner calmly walked to the cell door and then down the stone hallway to the site of his or her execution. These executions took place in the center of the arena floor, usually before large crowds.

I had been with many of these prisoners for the larger part of the three months. While I was in the same jail cell, I was not "with" them. I was not "with" them when they arrested me, and I didn't consider myself to be "with" them then.

The only people I was with were my team members, and I understood they were all dead. We were a five-man special ops team working in Europe when the authorities discovered our mission. My captors told me that I was the only member of my team to be taken alive. I didn't have any independent confirmation on this, but I believed it to be true.

The Special Ops assignment started when the new world leaders summoned our president to Rome for a mandatory meeting. Our officials, concerned about our president's safety, expanded the standard security team to include my team. Our stated mission was to protect the president during the time that he was in Rome attending this meeting, but our real mission was far more sinister.

I was not then and had never been a part of the presidential security team. Even on that trip I was not really a part of the security team. Our team's stated position on the security detail was a cover story concocted by Col. Black so that we could engage in our real mission.

Certain government officials had recruited my team and me for this special mission considered by all to be of the utmost importance for the future of the United States. Our team had been unceremoniously retired two decades ago, but now the government had a need for our special skills, so we were suddenly important again.

My team had successfully completed its assignment in Rome and was headed to a rendezvous point to meet with an extraction team when I was rendered unconscious. When I regained consciousness, I was in the commandant's office, propped in a chair. The commandant engaged me in a short conversation and then had me transported to that jail cell.

When they dumped me in that cell, I was still groggy from the drugs they used to render me incapacitated, so I stumbled to a spot near the back of the jail cell and sat down on the stone floor. The other prisoners wisely left me alone, so I remained on the stone floor until I regained my senses.

When I adequately regained my senses, I got to my feet and slowly surveyed my surroundings. I was not just trying to see where I was; I was also looking for a way to escape that cell. The cell was approximately fifty by fifty feet and was bordered on three sides by thick rocks with no openings or windows. The remaining side was totally covered with one-inch-thick bars spaced six inches apart, with a solid metal door approximately two feet wide by three feet high. They had placed the metal door in the center of the bars, and they had built it so that only one person at a time could exit.

There were numerous other cells located around us almost in a circular pattern. The outside wall was circular, and they had placed the cells around the outer walls with the center of the axis saved for the guards. The guards' room was approximately fifteen feet in diameter and was directly in the middle of the jail cells.

I was able to count most of the jail cells, and I believed there were approximately ten of these cells. Each cell contained about the same number of prisoners as my cell, so I estimated there were about one thousand prisoners waiting for execution.

As I continued looking for weaknesses in the prison, I was reaching the conclusion that any escape would be very difficult. The number of guards on duty, would make it difficult for me to escape alone. I could have used some help, but that wasn't available. I could have killed one guard or maybe two, but there were always at least five guards on duty, and without professional assistances the task of escape would have been difficult.

I was looking around at my fellow prisoners to see if any of them would be of assistance, but it was obvious that these prisoners were just regular civilians. I didn't see even one prisoner who I believed had any military background. I doubted that any of these prisoners had even killed a fly, let alone a fellow human being. It was obvious that these prisoners would be of no help to me. Even if they wanted to assist, they would only be a hindrance.

Where were my Special Forces buddies when I needed them?

I was unable to devise an escape plan, and I believed that time was running out on me. One sadistic guard looked right at me and laughingly said, "Tomorrow you will die."

I had no reason to doubt him, so I had to assume that I only had that night to come up with an escape plan. If I could not escape, and I was scheduled to die in the morning, I hoped this sadistic guard would be the one escorting me to the execution. I would kill him before I died.

This guard took the most pleasure in reminding the prisoners of their pending deaths. All the guards treated us like cattle going to the slaughter, but this guard was especially sadistic.

Some of the guards took pleasure in beating some of the helpless victims, and it was not just the men whom they beat. They didn't even spare the women in our cell. This one sadistic guard carried a cattle prod and got great enjoyment from shocking any prisoner he noticed was standing too close to the bars.

I had made myself a vow that I would kill this guard before I died. I wanted his death to be slow and painful, but I knew I would have to make it quick. I had made a metal shank with a breakaway handle so that after I stabbed the guard, I could break the handle off so that they could not remove the blade. I planned on sticking the guard in the neck, but the chest would also be acceptable.

My thinking may be foreign to you and maybe even repulsive, but it was simply a matter of logic, not emotions. I didn't hate this guard, but if I was going to kill one of them (and I was), then why not the most sadistic? He was a bully, and bullies deserve to be brought down.

I am going to share the rest of my thinking with you, just in case you are ever in a similar situation. What I am going to share with you could eventually save your life.

To complete my escape, I needed to create a diversion that would take all attention off of me. If I could stick a guard, it may be that in the confusion and their vain attempt to save his life, I could reach the door and thereby reach freedom.

If my desperate plan failed, then at least I had taken one of the enemies with me. I didn't plan on dying alone.

If you have any doubts about the wisdom of my plan, just let me assure you that it had worked on at least one previous occasion.

You, as civilians, are not expected to understand this logic, but the guards and I were all warriors, so we understood this line of thinking. They would take the same action if I were a guard and they were prisoners. A soldier can't become emotionally attached to our victims because emotions only will slow down our reflexes. We must deal only in logic, and all emotions must die if we are to be successful in our special missions.

I was remaining separated from the other prisoners so that I could work on my plan. I had taken a deserted spot on the floor near the back of the cell, and the prisoners quickly found out that they were not to approach me or engage me in conversation.

I did not want to be distracted from observing the guards because I knew that somewhere in their patterns there was an opportunity to escape. I just needed to have time to find that opening or weakness.

CONDITIONS IN THE CELL

The conditions in our cell were repugnant, to say the least. Three years ago the great earthquakes, which struck the entire world, destroyed whatever power systems there were in Europe. The world leaders had been unable to repair the entire electrical grid, so much of Europe remains without electricity.

The lack of power was especially bad in this dungeon. There were no windows, and the only air circulation was through the open doors, if the guards allowed any doors to remain open. At one time, there were fans and even air conditioning in this dungeon, but without power, they were useless. The air was stagnant, and the smell of mildew was at times overwhelming.

The days were extremely hot in Rome, and the nights were mostly down around freezing. During the days we sweated, and during the nights we froze.

Many days, as an example, I was soaked in sweat, and even the floor around me was damp. The guards often refused to give us water, so we were also dealing with dehydration. The stench of our body odor reminded me of a college football locker room during the halftime break of a hotly contested game with the windows and doors closed and the air-conditioning system broken.

Sometimes the odor was so bad I almost gagged as I try to capture whatever clean air was still available. I felt especially sorry for the young women who were trying to remain strong but obviously they were suffering greatly. Occasionally I saw one or two of them break down and start quietly crying, but for the most part, I was impressed by their courage.

The nights were even worse than the days because the temperature dropped to just above freezing. The stones were extremely cold, and in many cases the sweat from the heat of the day still permeated our clothes, adding to the chill factor.

The guards had blankets to give us, but they wouldn't bring them to us. The guard I described as sadistic brought the blankets to our cell and placed them on the floor just beyond our reach. We could see the blankets, but we could not reach them. The prisoners had handled this form of torture very well. I was impressed by how the prisoners supported each other. At night they gathered in groups and huddled together to share body heat. They always placed the most vulnerable prisoners in the middle and placed a wall of bodies around them. By vulnerable, I meant those who were on the edge of breaking emotionally and needed that extra support from the others.

I had been invited to join a couple of groups, but I would not become emotionally attached to anyone, so I remained in my little space and forced myself to endure the cold quietly. There was a time in the Special Forces when I was forced to endure very cold temperatures and was minimally affected by the cold, but now it was different.

Being as I was now seventy-three, I didn't seem to tolerate the cold like I used to. Some nights I shivered so uncontrollably that my fellow prisoners thought I was having a seizure. One night they thought I had gone into convulsions, so they approached me to render aid. I made it very clear that they were to leave me alone.

I looked forward to the hot, muggy days. Usually late in the morning it warmed up enough so that I could get a few hours' sleep, and sometimes late in the evening before the freeze started I could get a few more hours' sleep. That specific night I was shivering, but at least the cold was bearable.

I knew I was going to die the next day, and that didn't bother me. I knew when they captured me that death awaited. Even when I volunteered for this mission, I knew it was most likely a suicide mission. Death was always a part of life. You did what you needed to and let the rest take care of itself.

Tomorrow I would meet my fate on the floor of the arena.

I was not worried about tomorrow, for tomorrow would take care of itself.

I was thinking about tonight, not tomorrow. If I could have a final wish, it would be for some warmth so that my final night on this earth would be more bearable.

I guessed even this wish was going to be cruelly denied me, for I was still sitting on the cold floor, shivering and anticipating the dawning of another day.

INVADING MY TERRITORY

As I looked around me and survey the situation, I was impressed by the strength and determination of my fellow prisoners. They seemed to be genuinely concerned about each other, and there seemed to be some emotional bond between them.

I had overheard them talking to each other, and it was obvious from their conversations that they became acquainted after they ended up in this cell. I did not understand how people who were facing death could waste their time developing emotional ties. It was all going to end with their deaths so why waste time developing relationships?

No one seemed to be interested in fighting or trying to escape. They all seemed to be at peace with their pending executions. I overheard many of them say, "I will be going home soon."

Even when the guards called their names and they started the long walk out into the arena, they usually turned to the remaining prisoners and made the statement that I had heard so often. They almost always repeated the statement, "It's my turn to go home. See you soon." If it was not that exact statement, it was very similar.

In the past, I had seen men mentally break as they faced impending death. It was like they entered a dream world where reality was not present. I knew these people also must be snapping because they were delusionary in their belief that they were going home. They all got this serene look on their face, and a cloud of peace seemed to surround them. They walked out of the prison like they were meeting a bus outside that would take them to the land flowing with milk and honey.

I didn't want to rattle their little delusionary world, but the reality was they were going to meet a guillotine rather than a bus.

A few of the prisoners had tried to make conversation with me, but I refused to talk to any of the prisoners. I greeted each one who dares approach me with a hard glare and a cold shoulder. I had often seen them watching me, and I forced eye contact with them. It was not very long before they looked away. I had also seen a few of them talking in small groups, and they kept glancing at me, but only a few had the courage to approach me. No one has had that courage lately.

Until earlier that evening!

It was almost midnight, and the only light available was from the lantern the guards had at their desk. The flickering flames of the lantern cast an eerie light on the cell walls that often appeared as if someone was dancing on the walls of our cell.

I knew that it was a shadow of people walking about the cell, but it was funny how the mind works. Occasionally it appeared as if someone was approaching me, but when I looked up they were just changing positions. It was the shadows that provided the illusion.

That night, I saw two shadows that appeared as if they were approaching me. Logically I knew that it was an illusion, but it sure looked real. I continued to ignore the illusion until they sat down.

It was then I realize that two people had the audacity to violate my personal space, I was instantly angry. I angrily turned to them with all the hatred in me contorting my face into a violent mask conveying my intense anger, but they just ignored my anger and sat down. They not only were not leaving, but they were moving even closer.

I recoiled like a cornered animal. I was ready to strike out when I stopped and looked at this couple sitting next to me. I was used to reading the nature of a person, and I was hardly ever wrong. So often, my life had depended on my insight into the nature of other people. When I looked at this young lady, it was like a cloak of innocence was wrapped around her. There wasn't an inkling of fear in her eyes, only the innocence and the compassion in her spirit that came forth. I had not seen such compassion since the disappearance of my wife.

I continued to look directly into her eyes. The eyes are the window to the soul, and you can see who a person is through their eyes.

The cold, seething violence in my eyes was being met by the deep soothing love and compassion in her eyes.

For the first time in my life, I lowered my eyes and looked away.

I looked at her husband, and even then I was unable to detect any sign of fear. He was quietly but firmly supporting her as she tried to break through my violent barrier shielding me from the vulnerability of emotional ties.

Her eyes reminded me of the last time I allowed my emotions to become vulnerable. It was twenty-three years ago when I allowed my family to enter my private, scar-encrusted, emotional hell. I opened up at that time and began to lower my emotional defenses, and I became vulnerable to the love of my family.

I had started to live again and even enjoy life when suddenly something ripped my entire family from my grasp, along with millions of other people, who suddenly disappeared from this earth.

At my most vulnerable time when I needed my family, they suddenly left me, and I was once again alone. I determined at that time to never open myself up to any emotional ties, so I hardened my heart and became even more reclusive than before.

As I continued to look at this young couple, I begin to feel emotions stirring within me. I reburied all of my emotions three years ago, and now this couple was trying to dig them up and expose them to the world.

I felt as if I had to control my emotions and keep my emotional barriers in place, or I might become

11

vulnerable again. At the same time, my memory reminded me of the time I opened myself up to my family and enjoyed the feeling of love and emotional openness.

I was now fighting a personal battle within myself. I wanted to experience the love and compassion this couple was extending to me, but I got hurt every time I opened up. I also realized that we were all going to die soon so what good was it to have an emotional relationship? They should be thinking about their pending deaths, rather than an old man sitting in the corner of a cold jail cell.

While I was fighting this internal battle, she had continued extending her hand toward me, and she had just touched my hand.

I started to recoil, but something about her demeanor froze my hand in place. She was gently resting her hand on mine and waiting for a reaction.

As her hand rested on mine, I felt as if my wife had taken my hand. I was slowly feeling the emotional scars drain from my inner being, and I was starting to feel a dangerous vulnerability return.

My emotions were unwillingly being loosed.

This young lady who could not be over twenty-five years of age quietly said, "I am Brigette, and this is my husband, Andre."

I was not going to respond, so Andre said, "Our last name is Masson, and we are from the city of Nice, in France."

He continued on to describe a small house they had purchased a couple of years ago. He talked about how beautiful the cottage was and how it was so close to the beach.

I responded in a guarded voice, "That sounds beautiful."

He asked where I was from, and I told him California.

He said that he and Brigette met in California while they were both attending the University of Southern California. He said it was love at first sight for him, but it took a little longer for Brigette to come around.

He said he'd spotted Brigette in a physics class in which they were both enrolled. He immediately started a conversation with her and realized they were both exchange students from France.

He said their friendship grew until he finally proposed to her immediately after their graduation.

The tender and loving way he was talking about her touched me, and you could see the love they had for each other.

They married in a small family ceremony in France and then settled in Nice and were hoping to start a family soon.

As I was listening to this couple and witnessing their innocence, I could not imagine what they could have done to deserve death, so I point blank asked them. I looked at Andre and said, "What did you and Brigette do to deserve death?"

CONDEMNED FOR WHAT?

Andre looked at me and said, "Like everyone else, we were arrested for witnessing. Weren't you arrested for the same offense?"

I answered him, "No! They arrested me for attempted murder."

He said, "I thought you were one of us. I didn't know you were a criminal."

At that moment, I think I came to know how the thief on the cross felt as he hung next to the Holy Jesus.

This couple was so sweet, loving, and innocent that I did not feel I should be anywhere around them, yet even with that fact, they still accepted me as I was.

I was curious about what all of these people had witnessed that was deserving of death, so I asked them.

In response to my question, Brigette asked, "Do you mind if I start at the beginning so that you will understand the entire story?"

I answered her with a quiet laugh, "Sure. I think I can make some time. It doesn't seem like there is anything pressing on my schedule."

She gave me a little grin (just like my wife used to) as a reward for my attempt at humor, and then she continued with her story.

She said that while they were at the University of Southern California, someone had invited them to an on-campus Christian Club, and they both decided to attend.

They first heard about a man named "Jesus" at the Christian Club. The Christian Club was showing the series *Left Behind* by Tim LaHayes, and they were able to watch the entire series.

They found the series interesting but considered it to be totally fictional and completely illogical. It just did not make sense to them.

Brigette said that both she and Andre were Jewish by birth but raised in secular families, so they had never given any thought to religious things.

Brigette said things changed three years ago when millions of people suddenly disappeared. They remembered the *Left Behind* series and started studying the Bible. As they compared it to the news reports, they both became convinced that the Biblical account was true. If the Biblical accounts were true, then, Jesus was the real Messiah the Jews had been seeking.

They were so excited about their scriptural find that they just had to share the good news, so they immediately went to the local synagogue. What they found at the synagogue totally surprised them.

They found hundreds of other Jewish men and women from every known tribe gathered there sharing their newfound revelations about Jesus of Nazareth. Realizing that they had a life-changing truth, the members of the synagogue felt obligated to share their newly found truth. They started witnessing about Jesus to everyone who would listen, first to the Jewish families they knew, and then to anyone who listened.

She said it was after they started witnessing that the World Police Force began arresting anyone caught witnessing or even mentioning the name of Jesus.

Those who were arrested simply disappeared, and no one ever heard from them again. No one knew where the World Police Force took them or what the outcome of their arrests was, but these arrests just inspired them to witness all the more.

Andre said to me that they had been able to evade arrest for almost the entire three years, but they were finally caught in a police roadblock while they were sharing about Jesus in Rome.

Brigette said, "We are both willing to die for the truth, and we will not deny Jesus, our long-awaited Messiah."

When Brigette said this, I think the reality of the situation hit her. She and Andre were going to die for their faith, and this would occur sooner than later. I saw her eyes water up, and she reached out and took Andre's hand and just looked away.

Her eyes were not focused on anything, and there was a definite thousand-yard stare in her eyes. I had seen this same vacant stare in many soldiers as they entered a battle they did not expect to survive. It was almost as if they were looking at the past, present and the future all at the same time while still being unable to focus on any one of these.

I was going to leave Andre and Brigette alone so that they could share some precious time together before their executions.

Later that night Andre came to me alone and asked a very simple but troubling question.

He said, "I'm afraid for Brigette. I need to know if it is going to be painful."

I answered, "Fear will be a terrifying part of the ordeal. Death will be quick and painless, but the walk to the gallows will be terrifying."

I told him that Brigette would need all of his support and encouragement. I said to him, "Put your arm around her waist to help give her support. You believe in heaven, so talk to her about the beauty of where you are going rather than the death you are facing."

I told him, "Don't let her look at the guillotine. Keep her eyes on your face."

EXECUTION

Early that morning four guards came to our cell and called out Andre's and Brigette's names. I was very proud of them as they stood up and bravely walked down the stone hallway. Prior to leaving our cell, both Andre and Brigette turned to me and said, "It's time for us to go home."

As they were exiting the jail cell, Brigette placed her left arm around Andre's waist, and he ran his arm down her back. He was holding her around her waist and pulled her close to him. He was smiling and talking to her as she gazed up into his eyes. There was a total sense of peace around them.

As they reached the end of the hallway, they stopped just before they stepped out into the arena. Right at that moment, I saw Brigette's knees start to buckle. Andre caught her weight and supported her while she composed herself, and then they stepped out into the great arena.

In approximately three minutes I believed I heard Brigette's quiet but strong voice as she began to sing a song about her Jesus, and then all I heard were two dull thuds, and everything went quiet.

I trust they are home now.

CHAPTER TWO
MY LIFE

HANDICAPPED AND SCARRED

The night before Andre and Brigette's execution, they asked why I was in the dungeon. They assumed it was for the same offense as everyone else in the jail cell. They looked shocked when I told them attempted murder.

I had always had a question about destiny—specifically my destiny. Was I born to die in that dungeon facing the guillotine, or did I make choices that led to that fate? Did a higher power predetermine that I would commit the act that brought me here, and if so, what responsibility did I bear for these acts? Did I have any choice in my actions, or were the decisions made for me?

The other possibility was that while walking through life, I made choices based on specific circumstances and experiences that brought me to that crossroads. If the other possibility was correct then, I and I alone was responsible for my present circumstances.

These were all interesting academic, intellectual endeavors, but when you think about the circumstances I was facing, how or why really didn't matter. Did it?

I came to the conclusion that there were three things that shaped our psyche and set the parameters by which we lived and died. We had no control over the first two, but it was the third one that allowed us some control over our destiny. If my conclusions were right, then I bore a lot of the responsibility for my predicament, but fate also played a large part, and for that I did not take responsibility.

There were three things that I contended forged our lives and ultimately determined our fate. The first one was our environment that was determined by our birth. The second was our experiences within that environment, and the third was our response to that environment and those experiences.

I knew this was a simplified version of a complex theory, but I was an assassin, not a psychiatrist.

I knew that everyone processed their experiences differently, and each person was the sum total of their environment and their experiences. That was what made us individuals. I had some unique experiences in my life, but many other people lived in similar circumstances. Regardless of the similar circumstances, they evolved into totally different people from me and did not end up in that dungeon.

I will share with you three things that set my childhood apart from the other kids. These three things were: (1) I was born deaf, (2) I had a severe speech impediment, and (3) I was always smiling. These three circumstances may seem insignificant to you, but as you would see, they helped shape my life and determined my fate.

My mom gave birth to me at the Los Angeles County Hospital early one morning in the month of December in the year of our Lord 1944. I was born in a country that was caught up in the ravages of World War II and was completing the Manhattan Project, where we developed the first Atomic bombs. We dropped those Atomic bombs on Hiroshima and Nagasaki in August of 1945, thereby changing forever the balance of power in this world.

The European conflict ceased when Nazi Germany signed the Instrument of Surrender on May 8, 1945, and the Asian conflict ended with the dropping of two atomic bombs in August of 1945.

The world was obviously a mess, but my birth was normal, as reported by the doctors, and they gave me a clean bill of health.

While I was still very young, my family loaded our possessions into our old Studebaker and moved across the country to a small, rural town in upstate Michigan. It was a beautiful town with many lakes and surrounded by hundreds of slow-flowing rivers that traversed the woods and small rolling hills. I believed Michigan was the perfect place for a young person to grow up in, especially in the 1940s.

The war ended shortly after my birth, and our soldiers returned home to a country bolstered by the victory in the European conflict. There was an unmatched spirit of optimism and patriotism that flooded our nation after the war.

I grew up reciting the pledge of allegiances, started the school day with prayer, and believed in the United States as the grandest nation on the face of the earth. My parents raised me with the idea that some nations were desirous of destroying us and our beliefs, and it was everyone's responsibility to defend our great country.

INFORMATIVE YEARS

My earliest recollection of my personal life was when I was approximately three or four years old. I remember living in the back of a gas station located on a busy two-lane road in rural Michigan. I believe there was either a shed or a garage behind the station, but that is only a vague memory, and I am not sure it is accurate.

I remember a driveway on the right side of the station and beyond that some cherry trees, but even those details are vague. It is not that my memory was poor, but those things did not matter to me.

I remember the driveway because there were some fifty-five-gallon gasoline drums stacked next to the station. I remember those drums because I stood on top of the drums so that I could grab two electrical wires attached to the side of the garage.

My dad had previously checked the wires to make sure they were dead, but someone must have turned the electricity back on. When I grabbed those two wires, my sister told me that flames came out of my hands. She ran to my father yelling, "Fire! Fire!" My dad panicked because those drums contained gasoline, but all he could find was my blackened hands.

I have to admit that the spanking I received was worse than the electrical shock.

I also remember the cherry trees because I loved to climb the trees and eat the cherries. My mom and dad told me not to climb the trees, but that was where the cherries were. Needless to say, I continued climbing the trees and eating the cherries until the day I fell out of the tree and landed on a cement roller used to compact soil. I understand I received a concussion, but again I don't remember all of the facts.

I remember more about the inside of the gas station than I do anything on the outside of the station. There were two sections to the gas station. The front section was where my mother ran a small grocery store and where the truckers paid for their gas. The back section was where our family lived.

I have tried to remember what the back of the station looked like, but all I remember was the sofa. I remember it being in the middle the room, and I remember sitting on that sofa and feeling very safe. I don't know why I felt so safe on that sofa, but something must have happened to make me feel that way.

I remember sitting on the floor next to the sofa and playing with my set of Lincoln Logs and the cowboys and Indians my parents bought me. I loved the Lincoln Logs and would play for hours with them. I would build houses and make them into little cities that would be occupied by the cowboys and Indians. The cowboys and Indians had plastic horses that I could make them ride. I lived in my private fantasy world when I played with my toys.

I remember one day my mother became a little unnerved when she noticed I had made hanging nooses and had tied them to the rungs of the chairs. I had each of the cowboys dangling from a noose that tightened around his neck.

I don't remember what fantasy I was living, but I did receive a lecture from my mother about the sanctity of life. I took her lecture to heart and made sure I only hung the cowboys when she was not in the room.

When I was bored, I would venture into the front of the gas station where my mother worked each day. The truckers would enter the store to pay for their gas, and they would often buy candy or other items my mother stocked. My mom sold various items, which supplied us with extra money to supplement our living expenses.

I remember some of the locals buying gas at our station but mainly I remember the many truckers who frequented our store. I was totally intrigued by the large trucks, and I would greet every trucker as he entered our store.

My greeting each trucker did create a problem for my mother, but I will explain that in a few paragraphs.

Let's talk about playmates.

I don't remember any playmates except for my sister. I am sure there were other children in the area, but I don't remember them. I have no memory of any children coming to the store or any children living in the neighborhood. I don't even remember any other houses in the immediate area.

Sometimes I wonder why I don't remember any playmates. It's not that I missed them or even desired to be around them. It just seems strange to me that I don't remember even one. I wonder if I had a bad experience playing with other children at that age, and maybe I blocked it from my memory. I understand that children compartmentalize events they consider too painful with which to deal. Maybe I compartmentalized some bad experience, or maybe there just weren't any other children in the area.

Oh well. It doesn't matter. That is the way it was, and I just accepted it.

I enjoyed being alone, and for some reason, I didn't need anyone else in my life. The psychiatrist later defined this attitude as being a "loner" mentality. I never did decide if this was a mental disorder or a blessing. But life is what life brings.

I will go ahead and share some things that happened in my childhood that I did not understand at the time, but maybe these facts will help you to understand what I became.

SPIRIT OF REBELLION

The first thing I did not understand was how many times I would be engrossed in playing with my Lincoln Log set, and suddenly my dad would pick me up and spank me. After he spanked me, he would tell me to do something, and naturally I would do it.

Why did he spank me before he told me what to do?

He never spanked my sister first!

Why was I the only one he spanked first?

Why didn't he just tell me what to do?

I would have happily done whatever it was he wanted me to do.

A few years later he shared with me that he would ask me to do something, but if I were playing with my toys, I would simply ignore him. He said I would pretend like he wasn't even in the same room as me.

He said regardless of the number of spankings he gave me, I still just ignored him. He said he would sometimes ask me to do something five or six times before he would resort to spanking. He said he never could understand why the spanking never worked. His conclusion was that he was dealing with one of the most rebellious and stubborn children that he had ever met. He said he was determined to break my spirit of rebellion. He knew if he could not break my spirit of rebellion, this attitude would destroy me later in life.

After this talk, I stopped and tried to remember even one time when he told me to do something before the spanking, and I could not remember even one time. I had no idea what my father was talking about, but my mother seemed to agree with my father, and even my sister backed up their version.

During the time the spankings were taking place I never got mad or angry, and I never became bitter. I don't even remember thinking about these events. In my young mind, I just accepted life as it was. The spankings were just part of life, and so I just sucked it up and got used to them.

The spankings didn't hurt that much. I just put the pain out of my mind and went on with life. Some things in life you never really understand. It's just the way life is. Learn to deal with it, and get on with your life.

As my life turned out, the rebellion wasn't the only problem in my life. There was another major problem that bothered my mother even more than the perceived rebellion.

SPEECH IMPEDIMENT

The thing that bothered my mother most was I had a bad speech impediment. It seemed as if I was unable to communicate on a verbal level because I could not pronounce my words. The sounds that came out of my mouth did not make sense to anyone who was listening, including my family.

My mother knew that I would start school in a couple of years, and with my inability to speak clearly, my mother knew that I would take a lot of teasing. She wasn't even sure that the public school would accept me because of "my problem."

She later told me that I started trying to speak at a very early age, but my pronunciation was so bad that no one could understand what I was trying to say. Most young kids have a problem with pronunciation when they start trying to speak, but they grow out of it. I never grew out of it, and I never seemed to improve.

I guess my speech impediment caused my mother a lot of embarrassment in the gas station. I was so enthralled by trucks and truckers that whenever a trucker would enter the station, I would run up to them, yelling, "Truck, truck." My mom was extremely embarrassed because with my speech impediment, what came out of my mouth sounded more like a cuss word than "truck."

I remember one time specifically that I saw a young trucker enter the gas station. I ran up to him and started saying, "Truck, truck." The look on his face was priceless. His mouth hung open, and he was totally speechless. He just stared at me for what seemed like hours, and then he slowly turned to my mom, who was standing behind the counter with her face beet red. They just looked at each other, and no one said anything. He slowly turned around and walked out of the store, shaking his head.

She said the only good part about my speech impediment was that I had somehow formed the idea that if someone was smoking, they were going to hell. If someone came into the gas station smoking, I would walk up to them and say, "You're going to hell." She said luckily no one understood me, so they would just smile at me and finish their business. I don't know where I came up with the idea that anyone smoking was going to hell, but I did.

Mom told me that she worked with me for hours upon hours trying to improve my speech, but to no avail. She never gave up, but she also did not see any improvement.

SMILES
The third situation that appeared to be the problem was that I was always smiling and always seemed happy. My mom said I always seemed to have a half smile, half grin on my face, and I always seemed to be content. She said I never complained or made any demands, and I never seemed to have any needs. She said what bothered her was that I did not express any other emotions. Most of the children she had contact with showed anger, sadness, or hunger, but I never had those emotions, or I did not show them.

She told me that I just accepted life as it was, and I seemed to be content with the good as well as the bad. She said I was a very easy child to bring up.

Many of the family friends made various comments about the fact that I was always smiling. They would say to her, "Doesn't he ever cry, yell, or throw a temper tantrum?"

Mom would simply say, "No."

"Doesn't he ever demand your attention?"

Again she would say, "No."

Every time she would answer, they would say, "It's not normal for a child to always be happy. Our kids are not."

The funny part is they would say these things while I was in the room like I was part of the furniture.

The friends would look at me and then say, "He sure is different." They would sort of roll their eyes and look toward heaven when they made their observations about how different I was. They also elongated the word "different" and they seemed to hold on to the "-erent" for added emphasis.

At the time, I did not understand what word they were saying, but I always associated it with their look and the roll of the eyes. I don't think I knew at the time what "different" was, even if I could have understood the word. I knew something was strange, and it appeared to be me.

I knew they were talking about my smiling, and I knew something was bothering them, but I didn't care what they were saying. I was happy, and I was happy to be happy. Obviously it was their problem, and they should deal with it and not bother me. If being different was the cost of being happy, then I would be different.

I don't know what I could have changed because I did not know what made me different. I loved my life. I loved my family, I loved the trucks, I loved my Lincoln Logs, and I loved my cowboys and Indians.

DIAGNOSIS

There were three main areas that our family friends were concerned about, and they all had to do with me. They talked about me while I was in the room, and they treated me like I did not understand them or was incapable of comprehending the topic.

I did understand every word. I did not always know the meaning, but I figured out what they were saying. It is surprising what kids understand.

Many of the friends shared with my parents their thoughts and observations about me. I knew my condition concerned them, and I also knew they had the best interest of my family at heart. What seemed to concern them the most was seeing a four-year-old who was always smiling (without the other usual emotions), who could not speak clearly, and who always tried to maintain eye contact. They said I would look at their face and seemed to be looking at their mouths. They said most four-year-olds would look away from their faces after a period of time, but I locked my gaze on their faces.

I remember hearing the adults tell my parents that they believed me to be, "mentally challenged" and "severely handicapped." They all seemed to have the same opinion, as I heard this stated more than once. They all suggested that my parents should take me to a psychiatrist immediately to help determine the level of my handicap.

They always had such sad looks on their faces when they told my parents, and they always tilted their heads and looked down at me with this pitiful look. I did not understand everything they were saying, so I just kept smiling at them and playing with my Lincoln Logs.

We were a poor struggling family trying to make a living, so my parents and my sister had to go without many necessities so that we could save up the money to have me evaluated.

They found out that the University of Michigan had a program for financially strapped families, and after saving up some money, they made an appointment for me. The psychiatrist gave me a battery of tests that lasted all morning. I don't remember the tests or the other methods of evaluation, but I do remember that we were in his office or an adjunct room for most of the day.

Approximately one week later we went to his office, and he gave them the diagnosis. They had this conversation while I was in the room, and I do remember part of the conversation, but most of it were like a foreign language to me.

I remember the Doctor saying, "First I have some very good news for you. Your son's not mentally challenged." I believe the actual words he used were "not retarded."

He further stated, "All the tests indicated that your son has a very high IQ, and in fact he is very mentally gifted."

My father said, "Then what is the problem?"

The psychiatrist said, "Your son is deaf. Because of his giftings, he has been able to learn to read lips. So long as he is looking at you, he can read your lips, but if he has his back to you, he will not even know you are talking. The deafness is also the cause of his speech impediment. He cannot hear the pronunciation, so he has nothing to copy."

This diagnosis broke my father's heart because what he thought was stubbornness and rebellion was my inability to hear. All of the spankings I had endured were the results of my deafness, not rebellion.

My dad's shoulders were sagging, and he had this very sad look on his face. He looked at my mother, and she had the same look on her face, and it was like some unspoken words were passing between them. I could read lips, not minds, so I did not know what they were communicating to each other, but it seemed to be very intense and filled with sadness.

The psychiatrist interrupted this tacit interaction between my parents by saying a surgical procedure was possible, and it could improve my hearing, which in turn would help with the speech impediment. He suggested that this surgery takes place as soon as possible because there was already a level of psychological damage, and he wanted that damage kept to a minimum. He said, "The tests have not determined the extent of his psychological injuries, but I do know that he has learned to live in his private world, and he seems to enjoy that world."

He further said, "He is very young, so we cannot predict what direction these emotional injuries will take him, but there are four main areas that have already been affected."

I was sitting between my parents facing the psychiatrist and could understand everything he was saying. I missed part of my parents' responses because I could not see them clearly and I had to keep turning my head to see who was talking. It was strange sitting there knowing they were talking about me.

I knew my parents were asking about the injuries and what they could do to minimize the effects of those psychological scars.

He responded to their question by stating, "The first area is that he will always be a loner. The second area is that society's standards will not sway him. He has developed his own. The third area is that he developed the ability to ignore pain and will not let it affect him. The final area is that he will not show many emotions." He said I would always use my smile to mask my real internal feelings, as I had already been doing most of my life.

His final words were, "He will always be different." When he said this, he looked down at me with a very sympathetic look on his face. I will never forget that look, and I came to hate that look and the words that usually followed: "I am so sorry."

Why was he sorry? He had nothing to be sorry about unless he caused my problem, and I knew he did not.

The good news was my parents were able to arrange for the surgery, and during the following two years my speech did improve, but I still had a noticeable problem with my pronunciation.

BULLIED AND BEATEN

The next two years were pretty normal. There was nothing out of the ordinary, and life was settling into a very comfortable and predictable pattern. The next major event was the day I was allowed to enter public school.

I remember that day. I was almost six years old because my birthday was in December, and according to school policy a child started school after their fifth birthday. My birthday being in December meant I was almost one year older than my schoolmates, but it also gave me one more year to mature emotionally and physically.

I remember when my sister started school. It was two years earlier, about the same time that I had the surgery on my ears. I remember being so excited about starting school with her that I did not even think about anything else that night. I tossed and turned all night, and I was awake when my mom knocked on my bedroom door and told me to get up.

All night I thought about how it would be to play with other children my age.

Would I like it?

What would we do?

What should I do when I met other children?

I never thought, "What if they don't like me?" Rejection never entered my mind because I had never experienced rejection, and so why would I even consider this?

My heart was pounding with excitement as I got ready for school, but outwardly I appeared very unemotional.

I felt so grown up as I grabbed my Flash Gordon lunch bucket and started walking to school with my sister.

We arrived at school early, so I just started walking around, looking at the playground, the lunch area, and the classrooms. I was just getting familiar with my surroundings when I spotted three boys who seemed to be about my age.

My sister said, "Why don't you go play with them?"

I replied, "I don't know what to do."

She said, "Just walk up to the merry-go-round and get on it when you can."

I started walking up to the merry-go-round, and as I neared the boys, I started smiling. I smiled to mask my emotions, and I tried to appear friendly in hopes that they would accept me. I didn't want them to see my insecurities, so I just hid them.

I didn't try to get on the merry-go-round; instead I went to a nearby tree. I leaned against a tree, looking down at my feet (still smiling) and stood there shyly, hoping they would ask me to play.

One of the boys, whom I found out later was named Terry Milford, said, "What do you want?"

I said, "I want to pway."

They started laughing and saying, "He wants to pway. He wants to pway. He wants to pway."

I knew they were making fun of me, so I said, "Top it. Top teasing me."

Instead of stopping, they left the merry-go-round and surrounded me. Terry was the ringleader, and he started teasing me about my speech impediment and also about my ears, which I guess were rather large.

Their teasing was verbal at first, but then Terry began to flick my ears, and the others joined in.

They were flicking my ears and calling me names, so I pushed them away. It was at that time they started hitting me. While they were hitting me, they kept saying, "Top it. Top it" and then breaking into laughter.

Eventually, the hitting got harder and harder, as they found out I did not hit back. Finally, Terry doubled up his fist and hit me on the right side of my face, knocking me against a tree. As I got to my feet, all three of the bullies started hitting me and shoving me. I remember falling and hitting my shoulder on the metal bar of the merry-go-round.

The metal bar hurt, but I ignored the pain and once again got to my feet. I was still smiling, and I think this infuriated them as they increased the veracity of their attack.

One of the bullies suddenly fell to his hands and knees right behind me and the other two attackers pushed me. I remember falling backward. I remember feeling like my head was exploding as I hit my head against the metal merry-go-round, and then everything went black.

I woke up in the nurse's office, lying on a cot with a major headache. She placed an icepack on the back of my head and asked if I was OK. I tried getting up, but she made me lie on the cot and told me my dad was on his way.

My dad took me to the local emergency room, where the doctors determined that I had suffered a concussion. They kept me in the emergency room for a few hours, and then they released me, and my dad took me home.

My dad asked me, "Why didn't you fight back?"

My response to this question may be strange, but I never thought about fighting back. I didn't know what to do. In my private world, things like this never happened. I didn't even know what fighting back meant.

My dad saw my confusion and told me that fighting back meant that I would start hitting them back. He said, "When someone hits you or tries to hurt you, you can defend yourself. You do this by hitting them harder and faster, and you don't stop until they are running away."

My dad then got a very sad look on his face, and I think I saw tears in his eyes as he explained to me when it was all right to start fighting back. It was like he was explaining international rules of fighting that were appropriate for a society that I wasn't sure I wanted to belong to anymore. I had been so excited about starting school, and now for me the joy and excitement were over. The excitement did not even last until my first class began. If this was the way society was, why would I want to be a part of it?

My dad said, "Sometimes there are bullies who find people who are different or vulnerable, and they start picking on them. Those three boys are bullies, and for some reason, they decided to pick on you. They will continue picking on you until you fight back and show them you are not afraid."

I remembered the psychiatrist saying, "He is different," and I knew my dad was referring to that statement. I was sure glad that he did not say anything about my ears or the way I talked.

My dad continued and said, "Son, sometimes life can be cruel to those who appear different. There might be more occasions when you need to defend yourself, and on those occasions it is all right."

I understood what my dad was saying, but I didn't understand why this was happening to me. I just wanted some friends, but if friends hurt you like this and picked on you, then I made up my mind right then and there I did not want any friends. I had been alone most of my life, and I determined that it was safer for me to be alone.

I also developed a hatred for anyone who was a bully. I decided I would never allow anyone ever to bully me, and if I saw anyone being bullied, I would protect them and destroy the bullies for them. All of this was in my childlike mind, and I know now the mature logic was missing.

A couple of days later the doctors released me to go back to school. I could tell from the look on my mother's face and the extra-long hug she gave me as I left for school that she was afraid of what would happen.

I must give credit to my parents; they let me fight my battle alone. They let me face life's problems on my own. I was looking forward to going back to school because of the decisions I made, and even though I did not know the outcome, I was looking forward to the battle.

While I was out of school, I gave a lot of thought to my situation with the bullies. I knew from my dad's conversations that the bullies would not go away. I knew I would have to confront my fear eventually and confront the bullies that caused that fear. I decided to confront that fear as soon as I got to school. I also decided I would not stop fighting until I was unable to fight anymore. I knew that I would not give up, and no amount of pain would keep me from achieving what I needed to achieve in defeating these bullies.

With this resolve in my mind, I got ready for school. I didn't know what would happen, but I was ready.

As my sister and I approached the school, I saw the same three bullies standing next to the merry-go-round. I had played this exact scenario over and over in my mind, and I knew what I was going to do.

I put the same frozen half smile on my face and shyly walked out to the merry-go-round and leaned against the same tree I had leaned against originally. I did not look at them, but I kept my eyes locked on my feet. I could see the bullies out of my peripheral vision, but they did not know I was looking at them.

They sat on the merry-go-round and started calling me names and poking fun at me by mimicking my speech impediment. I pretended to ignore them by pretending to be shy and filled with fear. They left the merry-go-round and started to surround me. I forced myself to remain still and unassuming, but I was ready to strike. As they surrounded me, I quit smiling and looked them directly in the eyes with an unemotional, cold, hard stare.

I was totally unaware of anything but what I was going to do to these bullies.

Terry once again doubled up his fist and pulled back his arm to hit me. Before he could hit me, I stepped forward and started swinging at his face. I continued advancing on him while also taking the time to hit the other two bullies. I had never hit anyone in the face before, but I had to admit it felt good. As my fist continued to beat a pattern on his face, I got more confidence and started pressing the attack.

I concentrated on Terry until he turned to run away. Even when he started running away, I did not stop my attack. I chased him down and continued to hit him until he fell to the ground crying and curled up in a little ball like a baby. I jumped on him and hit him a few more times before I got up. When I got up, I saw his hand flat on the ground, so I stepped on his hand and fingers and twisted my foot grinding his hand into the ground. I wanted him to know that if he ever tried that again I would hurt him even after he gave up.

I then turned my attention to the other two bullies who were running away from me, and I chased them all over the playground until I caught each one of them. I beat them until a teacher intervened and saved them from further punishment.

The teacher took me to the principal's office, and to my surprise he just shook my hand and said to me, "I hope the fight is over now."

I said, "All right," and then went to class.

My immediate response to this fight was that I felt a new sense of confidence. I instinctively knew life had blessed me with a unique ability to fight. I knew life had blessed me with the ability to fight, but I also realized that I was better fighting alone. I did not need anyone to help me.

There was an unexpected benefit to this fight. The fight did not bring me any new friends (at this point, I did not want any), but it did elevate my status among my fellow kindergartners.

As a result of this fight, I became more isolated. My one attempt at having friends had turned out to be a disaster, so I determined that having friends was way overrated.

Some of the other students who had also been bullied by this trio made an attempt to approach me, but I quickly made it clear that I wanted to be alone.

The first time I noticed this was when I sat down at a picnic table for lunch. I opened my Flash Gordon lunch bucket, neatly arranged my food in front of me, and started to eat. Two students approached me and started to sit down. I never said a word; I just lifted up my eyes looked them in the faces, and gave each a hard stare as I slammed the lid on my lunch pail down.

They turned around and decided to eat somewhere else.

From that day on, the other students pretty much left me alone. They seemed to be afraid of me, or at least uncertain about what I would do. I let them think whatever they wanted to think, so long as they left me alone. I never made any attempt to be friends with anyone, and I began to enjoy the respect or fear they had of me.

My attempt to make friends had failed miserably, so I retreated behind the barrier of respect and/or fear they erected. I embraced my solitude and became more of a loner.

I was unaware of how deeply the scars of this experience had cut into me until I entered the tenth grade when these scars resurfaced.

INTERVENTION

My life was pretty much normal and uneventful from kindergarten until I reached the tenth grade. The only event worth mentioning is when we as a family moved from the east coast and resettled in California. Our move was a big change for me because we went from a small-time, rural town to a large city near Los Angeles. I went from a small school with few students to a large school with hundreds of students and every type of program you could imagine. There were more students in this school, but I still chose to remain a loner.

I had a chance to join the football team, but I didn't like the fact that winning depended on ten other players. I did not like relying on other people to fight my battles for me. Instead of joining the football team, I joined the wrestling team. They called it a team, but each one of us entered the ring alone, and we won or lost on our own merits.

I enjoyed a fair amount of success, and our team won a few tournaments, but while I was on the team, I was not part of the team. I was the official geek on the team because I was a top academic student, played an instrument, led the chess team, and never partied with the athletes. I was a part of many things, but I still kept the same distance from the other students that I started keeping in kindergarten.

Because of my athletics I was enrolled in the sixth-period gym class along with most of the other athletes. The reason they enrolled us in the sixth-period gym class was it was the last class of the day. After the class, we could just stay on the field and immediately practice for whatever sport we participated in.

This class was mainly athletes, but there were some other students in this gym class, mostly honor students who were maintaining an intense academic schedule. As you can imagine, there was a big difference between the athletes and the geeks.

These nonathletic students endured a lot of teasing, and on occasion I heard they were the victims of school bullies. I heard other students talk about these atrocities, but I never witnessed any of them.

All that changed one day as we were in the locker room getting dressed for PE.

A student named Jerry entered the locker room, went to an empty locker, and sat his books on the bench in front of him. Jerry was a rather small student, standing only about five foot one, and was quite skinny, weighing in at about 120 pounds. He played the clarinet in the school marching band and was a straight-A student always listed on the Dean's list. He was the classic geek, but he was very nice and always friendly.

Many times Jerry offered to tutor athletes who were struggling with their studies and took his personal time to make sure that they passed their classes.

I said hi to Jerry on many occasions, but I didn't know him as a person. I doubt if Jerry even knew my name or what sport I played. Jerry and I were not friends, so that is what made my reactions to this specific event so unusual.

Jerry was putting on his gym clothes when our star athlete walked into the locker room. His name was Brad, and he was a star football player. He was also one of the most popular students in school. The bad part about Brad was that he was an arrogant bully who often pushed around smaller students.

Brad walked up to Jerry and said, "Move your books."

Jerry started to move his books when Brad suddenly kicked the books off the bench and scattered them all over the floor. Jerry started to say something, but before he could get one word out of his mouth, Brad shoved him into the metal lockers.

40

When Jerry hit the metal lockers, I had a flashback to the metal merry-go-round and the pain I felt as I was knocked unconscious. I did not say anything, but I felt Jerry's pain and humiliation.

Jerry hit the locker so hard it knocked him to the floor. I could tell it hurt Jerry because tears came to his eyes. Jerry did not say a word. He quietly gathered his books and moved to another location away from Brad.

I looked at Brad, who was busy getting dressed for PE, and a small smile came on my face. I was fuming inside, but my exterior revealed nothing but a half smile. I lingered in the locker room until it was only Brad and me. I then walked up to him and quietly said, "Leave Jerry alone."

Brad's face got beet red, and he got right in my face and said, "I'll do whatever I want to do." He clenched his fists and leaned toward me in an attempt to intimidate me, but I just kept a frozen smile on my face and looked him directly in the eyes. My eyes narrowed until they were only small slits, and Brad missed the seething anger that hid behind my eyelids.

My actions only infuriated Brad even more, and he tried to shove me into the lockers as he had done to Jerry. As he reached out to shove me, I ducked under his arms. Using my legs and body, I threw a punch that hit him in the solar plexus, right where his ribs came together.

Brad immediately fell to the ground, gasping for some air. I reached down, grabbed his hair, lifted his face up, and looked him in the eyes. I simply said to him, "Leave Jerry alone." I then slammed his face into the cement floor, bloodying his nose. As he lay on the ground, I noticed his hand was lying on the ground, so I stepped on his hand and fingers and ground them into the cement. I then slowly walked out of the locker room and fell in with my classmates, who were busy running laps.

Eventually, Brad came out of the gym and joined our class. The instructor asked Brad why he was late, and Brad simply said, "I had a bloody nose." Brad was unable to explain why he also had two black eyes.

From that day on, I made it a point to take the gym locker that Brad had been using. I forced him to move his things to another area, but he never said another word to me. He never challenged me again, and he never bullied anyone in my presence ever again.

Jerry never knew what happened, but he was never subjected to Brad's bullying again. The interesting part is that later that year, Jerry spent some time tutoring Brad and made sure that he passed enough classes to continue playing sports.

Jerry was obviously the bigger man.

FEAR

Prior to the situation with Brad, there was another traumatic event that occurred when I was approximately twelve years of age that helped shape my future.

Our family moved into a small three-bedroom house on a very large lot. Our family had grown to include three boys and three girls. Even with three bedrooms, the house was still very crowded.

I shared a bedroom with my two younger brothers; my three sisters shared the other bedroom, and naturally my parents had their room. Things were going all right until my great-aunt got sick and needed to move in with us. She did not have any other family that was willing to help, so we willingly brought her to live with us. We believed if a relative needed help, the family helped. This was the way our family operated. If someone needed help, we reached out and helped them where we could. We did not have much in worldly possessions, but we always were ready to give to those in need.

We knew my great-aunt could not live in our small house, so to facilitate her arrival, my dad built a small brick house at the back of our spacious lot. He finished the bottom floor to give her a comfortable place to live. It had a kitchen, living room/bedroom, and a bathroom, and for a single person, it would be quite comfortable. The attic had a very high gable roof, so there was plenty of room for another person to live if they wanted to rough it.

The only entry into the attic was through openings at both ends of the building. My father left openings approximately three feet high by three feet wide at both ends. The opening on the south side of the building was left unsecured and open. He secured the opening on the north side with a makeshift door comprised of six wooden planks hinged at both ends and opening in the middle. The door locked with a cheap interlocking latch on the inside and another cheap latch on the outside.

The door was not perfect, as there were gaps on both top and bottom, and the gap between the two panels was approximately a quarter inch. During the summer, this was nice, as it always provided for a slight breeze but during the winter, it could be quite brutal.

To me it was the perfect bedroom. It was separate from the house, and if my parents agreed to let me move into the attic, I would be alone. I asked my parents for permission to move a mattress into the attic so that I could sleep there, and after much pleading they agreed to these new arrangements. I believe the overwhelming support given by my two brothers helped my parents make their decision, and so with the decision in my favor, the moving day came.

To gain access to the attic, I stacked two rickety ladders on top of each other. The first ladder had a small landing approximately two feet square on the top, and on this two-feet-square landing is where we placed the second ladder. The ladder system was not the best, but if I were careful, I could make the ascent.

I moved into the attic and started enjoying my solitude. It was a place where I could get away from people, including my family. No one seemed to bother me while I was there. My brothers were too young to climb the ladders, and my parents seemed to know how important the privacy was to me.

There was only one problem, and I have never shared this with anyone.

I was afraid of the dark. I was not just afraid; I was petrified with fear.

The back house, where I moved to, was surrounded by apricot trees, and it was extremely dark back there because there were no lights once you left the front house. When it was time for me to go out to my room, I would act real brave until I knew no one was looking. Then I would run to the back house, bolt up the ladders, dive through the doors, latch the cheap lock, and then sit on my mattress until my adrenaline stopped pumping.

I never shared my secret with anyone because my desire to be alone was so much greater than my fear of the dark. I just kept the fear internalized and masked it with a small smile.

I learned to live with this fear until one Saturday near the end of summer. The neighbor found a body in the alleyway between our yard and the neighbor's yard. I am here to tell you this shook up my young world when I saw the body covered up with a white sheet.

It was the body of a young lady who was a murder victim. The police determined her murder took place in another location, and the murderer dumped her body in the alley. The fact they murdered her somewhere else was of no comfort to me because I realized that the murderer was running free, and he had been within thirty feet of my room.

The police never solved the murder, so we knew the murderer was still running free. This fact stirred up many rumors in our neighborhood. The murderer had to be familiar with the area because the entrance to the alleyway was not visible.

The rumors quickly centered on a recluse who lived in an old house at the end of our street. He had access to the alleyway through his backyard, and no one would have seen him dump the body because it was late at night.

I was the paperboy for the neighborhood, and I delivered newspapers to him, but I had never even seen him. He lived in a small, unpainted, wooden house surrounded by a three-foot-high chain-link fence, and he always remained in his residence. No one could remember even talking to him, and very few had ever seen him.

His lot was just dirt with cactus plants scattered around his front yard. Someone started a rumor that you could occasionally see him scurrying among the cacti, performing some demonic dance during the full moon.

A nosy lady who lived across the street from this man said she heard that he had just been released from custody. She believed he had been confined in a hospital for the mentally ill. She believed the hospital was Patton State Hospital, and he was very deemed very dangerous.

All of the neighborhood children were warned to stay away from him and if he approached us, we were to run to the closest house screaming for help. It was hard for me to avoid him because I had to deliver his newspaper on a daily basis. I rode my bicycle as fast as I could when I was in front of his house and I threw the paper so that it would land right at his front door.

I never lingered near his yard.

The rumor quickly spread that the police suspected him of the murder but as of yet did not have enough evidence to arrest him.

Here are the facts that confronted me as a twelve-year-old dealing with an innate fear of the dark.

I knew there was a murderer on the loose and the rumors were they most likely lived at the end of our street. It also made sense to me that this murderer roamed the neighborhood at night because this was when he dumped the body near my room. These facts made my nightly trek to my room even more frightening, but still I did not share my fears with anyone.

A couple of weeks passed without incident, and I was starting to relax when something new shook my little world again.

I clearly remember the night when my fear once again turned to terror. It was on a Wednesday evening, and I know this because we had gone to Bible study at our local church.

The family started getting ready for bed, so I made my way to my secluded room, crawled under the blankets, and started to doze off when suddenly I heard a noise outside my little door.

The noise was unmistakable. It was someone climbing the rickety ladders that led to my door. I thought it might be my dad, so I waited for him to say something. He didn't say anything, so I knew it wasn't my dad. Terror gripped me as I realized a stranger was on the ladders. It was obvious to me that he was looking through the small gaps in my makeshift door.

I knew the person was lingering on the ladder because I could hear the ladder continually scraping against the brick wall. My heart was pounding as I knew he was peering through the door, and with my mattress only two feet from the door, I could almost hear him breathing.

To this very day, I can still hear and feel his breath as it made its way through the gaps in my door. I just lay there, pretending to be asleep, hoping that he would go away and leave me unharmed. Eventually, I must have fallen asleep because the next thing, I remember, was waking up and seeing sunlight shining through the gaps in my door.

I never said anything to my family about my late-night visitor, because I knew they would want me to come back into the house with them. The problem was this person returned night after night, and I could not tell anyone. I endured this torture because I loved my solitude perhaps even more than my life.

I wish I could accurately portray the intense fear that gripped me every night and the emotional torture I endured as this antagonist stalked me every night. He would spend hours peering through the gaps in my door while I would lie in bed, frozen in fear, waiting for him to leave. Eventually, I would fall asleep from pure exhaustion, and in the morning, he would be gone.

The emotional strain was so bad that one night as I got ready to go out to my room, I decided that I would not let this man torture me anymore. I decided to take drastic action that very night. It was the same mindset I had when I decided to fight the bullies in kindergarten so very many years ago.

I remember this particular Tuesday evening very clearly. I decided to make everything seem as normal as possible so as to not raise this man's suspicion about what I had in mind. I ran out to my room as always and quickly made my way up the ladder and jumped into my room.

I shut the door, but I did not lock it. I laid the latch over the eyelet rather than in it, and then I placed my pillow under my blankets so that it would appear as if I was in bed. I then took a position crouching next to the door and waited. I was waiting for my antagonist, who climbed the ladder every night, to appear so that I could put my plan into action.

Sure enough, within twenty minutes I heard him climb the ladders, and I knew he was just outside the door. I waited for an agonizing five minutes, and then in sheer desperation I kicked the door open and jumped on the man who had been terrorizing me for weeks.

As I exited the door, I missed the rung on the ladder and fell to the ground. I immediately jumped up and turned to confront my antagonist, but to my surprise (and relief) no one was there.

I looked all around me to see what had happened, and I noticed a broken limb on the apricot tree that would rub against the ladder when the evening breeze would come up. I felt foolish when I realized a broken tree limb blowing in the evening breeze was the reason I had experienced my terror. I had been terrorized by something that did not exist, and it was only the fear caused by my imagination that was real.

I started thinking that if there was no one on the ladder, then my fear must radiate from my imagination. I realized that it was my imagination that caused my fear. I realized that only after I confronted my imagination did I overcome my intense fear.

I thought about the other things in my life that brought fear. I wondered if they were also a figment of my imagination. My mind immediately went to the recluse who lived in the rundown house at the end of our street. Everyone was afraid of him, yet no one had ever met him. I determined I was going to meet him and find out if he was dangerous or if the neighbors were all afraid of their imaginations fueled by the rumors.

Like I said earlier, I was this man's paper delivery boy. I had always made it a point to get the paper as close to his front door as possible as I sped by his property. I usually got the paper right next to the door so that he would not have to leave his house, but today was going to be different. Today I was going to throw the paper just far enough away from the front door so that he had to come outside to retrieve it.

After I had thrown the paper, I hid behind a tree just outside his fence and quietly waited. After about twenty minutes, he opened the door and tried to reach the paper. He could not quite get to it, so he finally opened the door and after looking around, he stepped outside and swiftly grabbed the paper and started to retreat back into his home.

I quickly stepped out from behind a tree and simply said, "Hi." He jumped back into his home, and I heard the locks snap shut as he secured his front door.

I repeated this exercise every day for two weeks, each day placing the paper further and further away from the door. Every day when he would appear I would once again say hi, and once again he would quickly retreat back into his home without saying anything.

After two weeks, he finally said hi before he disappeared into the safety of his home. It took me almost two months before he ever said anything more than hi, but eventually he looked at me for a while before he went back inside.

I started asking him short questions that he could answer with one word, and eventually he even started talking. After many short conversations, I found out that he was a nice old man, but he was dominated by fear. He was afraid of everything and everybody, so he lived sequestered behind the walls of his home.

His sister brought food and supplies to him because he was so petrified of people that he was afraid to leave the perceived safety of his home.

I realized that I had one thing in common with this poor man. We were both prisoners of our fears and rampant imaginations. He was a prisoner in his home, and I had been a prisoner in my attic.

The sad part was the neighbors were also prisoners of their fears because they were afraid to walk near his house at night. Everyone was worried about this nice old man because they let their imaginations control them.

I decided that night that I would never again be a prisoner of fear. The only way to overcome fear was to confront it. The only way I defeated the bullies was to confront them, and the only way I defeated my fear of the man on the ladder was to confront him.

My reasoning at the age of twelve was the only way to defeat fear was to immediately confront that fear and control my imagination. I never discussed this with anyone, but I made a decision that night that would dictate my response to "fear" for the rest of my life.

CONFRONTING FEAR

The willful decision I made that night would affect the rest of my life. I decided that anytime I felt fear, I would immediately confront it. The only way I could defeat my fear was confronting it.

I viewed "fear" as an opponent that I had to challenge and defeat. I then embarked on a mission designed to overcome all of my fears, and if I were successful, then I would finally be free.

The problem is I overcompensated, and I became obsessed with confronting all of my fears. I came to realize that man's greatest fear is the fear of dying. Dying is the ultimate crossing over into the unknown and the final journey anyone would ever make. I remember someone saying, "Life is the only trip you will ever make that you are guaranteed not to live through."

The fact that I believed fear of death was the ultimate opponent meant that my belief drew me toward anything that could result in my death. The higher the risk, the greater the adrenaline rush. The closer I could come to death and still live brought the largest adrenaline rush and provided the adrenaline high that I so desperately sought.

As a result of my experiences and my reactions to them the only battles, which mattered to me, was when life and death hung in the balance. This psyche shaped the various choices I made in my life, and this psyche brought me to this point of death. Whether I die tomorrow or not doesn't matter. What matters to me is that I have conquered the fear of dying. I embrace tomorrow with the same enthusiasm that I embrace today.

While I was on an assignment in Mexico, a compadre gave me a ceremonial knife with the following inscription on it. This inscription reads, *"Vivir como se puede y morir como se debe."*

This inscription became and still is my life's motto. Tomorrow I will truly understand the last half: *"morir como se debe"*. I will die with the same dignity that I have lived. I will die like a man.

CHAPTER THREE
MILITARY DUTY

EDUCATION

In tenth grade, when I defended Jerry, I never imagined how closely our paths would intertwine.

The school system was just beginning to come to grips with the fact that many "gifted" students were not challenged by the current educational system, so they were investigating new ideas to stimulate these elite students.

My school district was no different from the others, but the idea they came up with was novel for that time in history. They selected three gifted students based solely on their IQ tests and enrolled them at the local state university.

The officials selected Jerry, a girl named Betty Jo, and me for this pilot program. At first they enrolled us during the summer session to judge how we would do in this new environment. They enrolled us in two classes each, and mine happened to be chemistry and physics.

I enjoyed these classes and managed to get A's in both classes. Based on my success in college, I skipped my eleventh and twelfth grades and became a college student. After two and a half years, I graduated with a double major in chemistry and electrical engineering.

I was unaware of how this seemingly minor event in my life would so drastically affect my future and my eventual occupation.

During the time I was in college, I became even more of a loner, not by choice but by circumstance. All of my friends—both of them—were still in high school. My fellow college students were three or four years older than me, so we had very little in common.

To fight boredom, I started taking classes in martial arts, specifically a form of competitive judo. I became very proficient at judo and started entering local and national tournaments. I soon earned a reputation as a martial arts expert and enjoyed the respect that came with those titles.

I graduated from college when I was nineteen and soon faced the mandatory enlistment in a branch of the military service.

I decided to join the United States Marine Corps, and on my nineteenth birthday, I arrived at the Marine Corps Recruit Depot in San Diego, California.

MILITARY DUTY

They assigned me to Platoon 363, and I started a thirteen-week odyssey of training where I would earn the right to call myself a marine.

I finished second in my graduating class, and they assigned me to Camp Pendleton for infantry training.

It was during my infantry training that I began to hear about a very special company of Marines called Force Recon. The Marine Corps stationed the First Force Recon at Del Mar, California. While I was going through boot camp, I witnessed many parachute jumps and was intrigued by what I saw and the many heroic stories I heard about this unit.

I knew these marines were a very elite Special Forces Unit. They were highly trained in airborne, scuba, and various other methods of insertion and were used to support the other ground units.

I remember the first time I saw the unit jump at Camp Pendleton. The sound of the approaching aircraft sounded like thunder, and when they came in view, there were at least 15 C-130s flying in formation. As they passed over the landing zone, you could see the marines exiting the planes, and then the sky was blanketed with parachutes as wave after wave filled the sky.

I was unable to see the actual landing, but my heart was beating fast as the jumpers disappeared over the horizon. That day I determined if I ever had a chance to join this elite band of warriors, I would immediately jump at the chance.

As fate would have it, my chance came during the last week of advanced infantry training. Our First Sgt. announced that the First Force Recon would be hosting tryouts on the following Saturday for those who had aspirations of becoming a Force Recon Marine.

I immediately volunteered and was instructed to report to the base of Old Smokey on Saturday morning at 6:00 a.m.

Everyone at Camp Pendleton knew where Old Smokey was because all of us at one time or another had had to run up the grueling trail leading to the flagpole.

This particular mountain was known as Old Smokey because most mornings the fog from the ocean covered our view of the top. The slope leading to the top of Old Smokey had to be at least a 60 percent grade. It took every ounce of endurance and strength one had to run to the top, especially without stopping.

The morning of the tryouts, I arrived at the base of Old Smoky at approximately 5:30 a.m. just to make sure that I was able to warm up before the tryouts started. There to greet us was Gunny O'Malley, who was already a legend among Force Recon. He was a short, stocky marine of Irish descent covered with tattoos from his neck to his ankles. In addition to the tattoos, he was always chomping on this unlit stogie that dangled from his battle-scarred lips.

Gunny O'Malley had steely, cold blue eyes that seemed to cut to the very depth of a man's soul, and every warrior knew that you did not mess with the Gunny. His command presence was awesome, as his very demeanor demanded total commitment, and most marines would sacrifice their lives just to please this legendary warrior.

At exactly 6:00 a.m., the Gunny ordered all of us to fall in behind four lines of knapsacks. After we had fallen in behind the knapsacks, Gunny O'Malley stood in front of us, silently sizing each one of us up. Then he said, "You will put on the knapsack at your feet, and at my command you will run up Old Smokey and fall into a formation at the base of the flagpole. Anyone who stops running for any reason will be eliminated. Am I understood?"

We all answered, "Yes, sir," and then put on the knapsacks that weighed approximately twenty-five pounds. The weight was very light compared to what we usually carried, but usually we did not have to run up a mountain.

I looked at the ground as I focused my thoughts on the grueling run before me, determined that I would be one of the first marines to reach the top.

There were a couple hundred of us who started running up Old Smokey that morning with the ultimate goal of becoming a Force Recon Marine. The first one hundred yards of this test shattered many a marine's dreams of joining this special group.

The first one hundred yards included an 80 percent incline. The incline then leveled off for approximately twenty feet, and then started the final half mile to the flagpole. The final half mile was an unbroken 60 percent incline, and it was this last incline that defeated many of the lesser prepared marines.

As we reached the first plateau, I saw some marines already beginning to fall out. Some were vomiting, and others had dropped their knapsacks. I knew there was no way these specific marines were ready for the tryouts.

I remember my quadriceps starting to burn as I reached the first plateau and then started the main incline to the flagpole. As I neared the top of the final slope, the burning in my legs had turned to pain, and I had to control my breathing as my tortured lungs begged for oxygen.

I was in the top ten as we reached the flagpole, and rather than sit down as some of the others did I remained on my feet and tried to regain my strength. My legs felt like rubber, so I walked in a circle around the flagpole until my breathing returned to normal and my legs felt like they could once again support my weight.

By the time my body returned to normal (as much as possible), the last of the marines had reached the pole. There were at least sixty marines who were not able to make the run, so Gunny O'Malley was in the process of dismissing them.

As soon as the last marine reached the flagpole, Gunny O'Malley ordered us to fall into formation. He congratulated us on our accomplishment and then ordered us to run down Old Smokey and fall in near a large oak tree that afforded us the only shade for over half a mile.

As I fell in near the tree, I saw a pile of knapsacks stacked on the ground a short distance from where we were standing. In the back of my mind, I knew that this was not a good sign, but I tried to ignore my premonition.

I tried to convince myself that the knapsacks were for a new group of recruits, but I knew that it was only hopeful thinking.

Gunny confirmed my thoughts as he told us each to drop our knapsack and grab another one from the new pile. As I grabbed the new knapsack, I immediately found it to be heavier. I could not judge if the pack were really heavier or if it just felt that way because of my fatigue.

My back was already hurting, and my legs once again felt like rubber, but at least I was starting to regain my breath. I was going to say I got my second wind, but I think I was already on my third or fourth.

I didn't know what Gunny O'Malley had in mind, but I knew it would be grueling.

The Gunny once again stood in front of us and with a sarcastic sneer said, "You ladies haven't even started yet. What you will go through today will make hell look like a resort. Give up now, and save yourself some pain. You are not going to make it anyway!"

He then started walking up and down the formation and would order each marine to drop and give him fifty pushups. Some of the marines dropped their knapsacks to do the pushups, and immediately an instructor would grab them and demand to know, "Who told you to drop the knapsack?"

The marine would respond, "No one, sir," and the instructor would grab the knapsack, put two or three more rocks in the pack, and make them put it back on. I know that the extra rocks added ten to fifteen more pounds to the weight, and you could see in the eyes of the marines that they were giving up.

As we were doing our pushups, Gunny O'Malley would stand on our knapsacks, yelling for us to quit and telling us that we would never make it as Force Recon

Marines. A number of marines did walk off, but the majority remained.

I believe there were about 120 marines remaining after the pushups, and when we returned to the formation, my estimate proved to be accurate.

Gunny O'Malley grabbed a knapsack that was obviously heavier than ours and told us that we would once again run up Old Smokey. This time, however, he would be running with us, and he would be carrying a pack that was fifteen pounds heavier than ours. He stated that he would eliminate any marine who arrived after him. There would be no exceptions.

Gunny's knapsack had to weigh at least fifty pounds, but we all knew that it would take everything we had to reach the top before him. As I looked around me, I could see a number of marines with their shoulders slumped and their hands hanging down. It was obvious that they had given up, and it was only a matter of time until they dropped out.

Gunny O'Malley changed his tone of voice and almost sounded like he cared about us and the pain that we would endure. He quietly walked up and down the line and told each marine, "There is no shame in dropping out. Just drop your pack, and walk away. Why take the pain when you can't make it anyway? You can always try again later."

He made it so easy to drop out that at least thirty more marines dropped their packs and walked away. There were under one hundred marines remaining as we started the run to the top.

Gunny O'Malley set a blistering pace as he tried to make each marine drop out. I started right next to Gunny so that I could keep my eye on him. I soon decided that I needed to get ahead of him by as much space as possible because I figured he would really speed up the pace during the final fifty yards.

The pain started back up as soon as we left the flat land and started our climb. This time the pain was more severe. The best that I can describe this pain to you is it felt like I had two Charlie horses, one in each leg. At the same time, my legs were burning. It felt like someone was pushing a white hot branding iron into the middle of both quads while I was trying to breathe through collapsed lungs.

I put everything I had into this run and was able to reach the flagpole approximately twenty-five feet ahead of Gunny O'Malley. On the run down, I also determined I would reach the flat land ahead of Gunny O'Malley.

I could see other Force Recon Marines grading us, so I figured that one of the parameters of success was whether we put everything into the tryout or just tried to get by.

Once we were in the formation, I realized that only fifty marines, were still standing and that everyone else had dropped their packs and returned to their units.

As I stood trying to get my breath, I realized that it was only 7:30 a.m., and the testing had just begun.

Genny O'Malley said, "All, you have done so far this morning is earned the right to begin your quest to become a Force Recon Marine. The test will start in five minutes. You are to get some water and fall in next to that tree."

As we got a drink of water and washed the dirt from our faces, we realized that this was now make it or break it time. Our futures in the Marine Corps would depend on what we did during the next twenty-four hours.

During the rest of that day and most of the night, we were subjected to tests that would measure our resolve, our physical stamina, and our mental strength.

We endured all of this as we sought the right to begin training as Force Recon Marines.

I made it through the test that day, and three days later I was notified I had passed the test and earned a position with a Force Recon Unit.

TRAINING

A week later, I graduated from the infantry training regiment and received my orders to report to Fort Benning, Georgia, for jump school.

The jump school was only three weeks long, but the exhilaration I felt as I prepared to board the C130 for my first jump was an experience I would never forget. I remembered all of the jumps I witnessed at Camp Pendleton, and now I was not an observer. I was a participant. I would be one of the many chutes deployed behind the C130's, and I would earn my wings.

I was the first jumper in the line, and as I stood ready to exit, my adrenaline was flowing, and it felt good. When the jumpmaster tapped me on the shoulder and I leaped out of the plane, it was a feeling that words could never describe. The exhilaration was beyond description, and that day I became even more addicted to the adrenaline rush.

The first time I had felt such an adrenaline rush was in kindergarten when I was getting ready to face the three bullies, and that day in kindergarten I knew I loved the feeling.

The day I leaped out of the attic door to face a "murderer" only increased the addiction, and now I was being paid by the marines for my addiction to adrenaline.

Through these and other experiences, I realized that the closer to death my experiences brought me, only increased the adrenaline high.

Death was and still is the ultimate opponent.

After graduating from jump school, I was assigned to Coronado Island, California, for some training with the Underwater Demolition Training Unit (UDT). After graduation from the UDT training, they next sent me to the Redstone Arsenal in Huntsville, Alabama, for specialized training in explosives, specifically nonmilitary.

The Anarchist's Cookbook was the title of the textbook used in our class in Alabama. It was the textbook used around the world by every terrorist organization.

After we had finished the basic textbook, we moved to more advanced formulas, where my education in chemistry greatly enhanced my intrinsic talents. It was at this time that my advanced education in chemistry began to separate me from the others in my class.

Many of my fellow students were not in the military. They worked for covert companies who in turn were hired by our government to engage in clandestine activities. The warriors were often deployed throughout the world, performing assignments that were highly secret. I was intrigued by these warriors, though we never talked about who they were or what they did. This topic was strictly off limits, and no one violated this code of conduct. It was at this school that I earned my nickname Boom-Boom. It was also where I earned my reputation.

Many people would assume that the nickname Boom-Boom was rather standard for someone with advanced training in explosives, but my name came through a special practicum that I will now describe.

The instructors separated our class from the other training classes, and they transported us to a secret location deep in the woods of Alabama. We were still on the base, but this location was only accessible by driving down a dirt road and through many secured checkpoints manned by non-uniformed, highly armed warriors.

Once we were in this secured location, we were informed that this phase of our training would include the fine art of placing booby traps in vehicles with the intent of eliminating the drivers.

We went through three days of instruction, and then each of us was assigned a vehicle with a mannequin sitting in the driver's seat. Our assignment was to design, build, and install an explosive device that would eliminate the target.

We were given two days to complete this assignment. After the two days, the devices would be detonated and graded by our instructors and fellow students.

I, along with my fellow students, finished our assignments, and on the third day, we gathered together to witness and judge each person's device.

One by one the devices were detonated and critiqued. The detonation of each device was accompanied by a loud explosion and a huge fireball and elicited the cheers of our classmates. It was obvious from the mangled wreckages and the charred, mangled mannequins that each device would have been very successful. In each instant, the device eliminated the target.

When it came time for me to detonate my device, I triggered the detonator. My fellow students and instructors became very quiet because all they saw or heard was a couple of muffled explosions, and two windows on the car blew out.

If you have ever been in a similar macho environment, you will understand the immediate mocking and teasing that I endured. There were many comments that included the word "wimp," and some referred to my manhood but I just looked at them and smiled.

In response to their teasing, I just responded that they were nothing but crude bombers, and they should just watch they would observe what a professional could and should do. I also reminded them that the car they gave me to set my device in was a 1963 Chevy Impala and that I was a car lover. That particular Impala was one of my favorite cars.

The instructor led us to my vehicle, and the class inspected the results of my device. The first thing they noticed was that the device had severed the mannequin's head from the body, and the head was lying neatly on the floor below the front passenger's seat.

My device was obviously a kill shot, and in that context was very successful.

The second thing they noticed was that both severed feet of the mannequin were still on the floor directly in front of the mannequin.

The instructor asked me to explain the rationale behind my design. I told him that I used shape charges that formed a cutting edge at a predesigned distance from the explosive. I chose the specific shape charge that formed the cutting edge somewhere between four and fifteen inches, and I placed it at the base of the driver's seat. After I had placed this device, I connected it to the starting switch so that when the driver started the car, this portion of the device would explode, severing his legs at the ankles.

I told him that when the driver lost his feet, he would naturally lean back in his seat, purely out of shock. The second device, which I installed at neck level, would then detonate, severing his neck and removing his head.

I told him the two detonations guaranteed a professional and neat job, and after some slight repairs, the car could still be driven.

I told them my intent was to eliminate the target with minimal collateral damage, and as they could see, I accomplished the goal.

I then continued making disparaging comments about their crude methods. They made many statements about my being a psycho, and then they gave me the nickname Boom-Boom because it took me two explosions to accomplish what they did with one.

As Rodney Dangerfield said, "I get no respect," but I noticed the instructors examined the Impala and the mannequin and took detailed notes. A short time later I saw a couple of important men being escorted to the Impala, and then they left the area.

This nickname has remained with me even unto this day. Some people call me by my nickname because they have heard others use it, and some because they were part of this team, but people will never know who is who.

I attended many other schools ranging from sniper to survival before I finally was qualified to be called a Force Recon Marine.

I was looking forward to serving with the Force Recon Units and embarking on a fulfilling career with the United States Marine Corps when life's circumstances took a different and unexpected direction.

NEW DIRECTIONS

The change in my life started on a Friday morning at about 10:00 a.m. when our company's first sergeant contacted me and told me that Major Toole wanted to see me in his office. I was rigging parachutes at the time, so I finished the one I was packing, signed the paperwork, and reported to Major Toole's office.

Major Toole introduced me to two men and then discreetly left the office.

The two men never told me who they worked for, but I assumed it was the CIA or a similar organization. All I really knew was that they were representatives of a highly secret branch of the government, and they wielded great authority and tremendous power.

They told me that they were forming a highly secret team of specially trained Special Ops soldiers who would work deep undercover. They would be called upon to perform extremely dangerous missions both within the continental United States and also abroad. This team would operate as civilians, and if compromised and captured, the government would deny any knowledge of the team or their mission.

My adrenaline immediately started flowing, and I have to admit that I was totally intrigued by this whole scenario and the clandestine nature of the team, so I impulsively volunteered for this mission.

They told me to wait and think about it for the next three days, and if I still wanted to volunteer, there would be a black 1965 Ford waiting for me outside the main gate at 6:00 a.m. They said that once I volunteered for this team, there would be no turning back, and my future would consist of this team.

I thought about it, and on Monday morning I was standing outside the main gate at exactly 6:00 a.m. with all my gear packed, per their instructions.

The Ford picked me up and transported me to a small, private airport approximately two hours' drive from my military base.

There was a small amphibious airplane on the dirt runway with the single engine running. After I had climbed aboard the plane, it started taxiing down the runway, and I quickly left my past behind. There was no conversation or greeting by the pilot—just a revving of the engine as we took off.

We flew for five hours and then landed on a small desolate lake deep in the rugged mountains of Montana. I believed we were northwest of Billings, Montana, because I saw a rather large city to the east of our flight pattern, and the only city I knew of that size was Billings. There was also a large plateau with an airstrip on it just south of the city, and I knew Billings had such an airport.

After we had landed on the mountain lake, the pilot taxied to a dock where three men were waiting. They escorted me to a log cabin perched on the side of the mountain overlooking this very secluded lake. I quickly surmised that this was a hunting and fishing lodge and because of its isolated location was perfect for our secretive meeting.

The mountain setting and the clandestine nature of the meeting seemed so surreal that I thought, "I must be dreaming." The entire situation was more befitting an action novel rather than a real-life experience. I expected to wake up from this dream or hear a movie director yell, "Cut," at which time I would find out I was still with my Recon Unit.

I came back to reality when a man who introduced himself as Col. Black entered the room. Col. Black thanked us for volunteering for this Special Ops team and told us he would be our main contact and would personally initiate all future communication.

We spent the next two hours getting to know each other, sharing our areas of expertise, and forming one cohesive team.

For the next three weeks, we participated in numerous field exercises that highlighted each of our specialties and made us depend on each other. At the end of that time, we were comfortable with each team member and were ready for the next assignment.

Col. Black advised us that we were officially separated from our active duty units and were reassigned to various reserve units. Specific reserve units were selected so that we could get additional training without calling attention to ourselves, and this would also provide a cover story to our employers when we were on assignments.

At this point, the official meeting was over, and after another week of hunting and fishing, I returned to civilian life and was assigned a job in the aerospace industry.

CHAPTER FOUR
CLANDESTINE MISSIONS (SPECIAL OPS)

Col. Black notified me that I was hired by a company in the aerospace industry. Just prior to my leaving the hunting and fishing lodge, I was handed a piece of paper with the company's name on it. I was told to report to Mr. Harrison, who was the Director of Research and Development for this company.

On the surface, this company was involved in designing and manufacturing potentiometers and dual in-lines. The specific division I was assigned to was a covert operation center used to provide cover for the various agents embarking on covert assignments.

In between covert assignments, we did research on various projects and were very instrumental in developing a new dielectric material used to print capacitors. At the time I was working on this project the industry was only able to print two or maybe three capacitors on top of each other. The industry needed a thinner dielectric material to facilitate the advancement of this technology.

We were on the verge of developing such material when Col. Black notified me and three co-workers that we were scheduled to take a vacation. The vacation would be a trip to Nigeria, West Africa, Liberia, Egypt, Jordan, Israel, France, and then Germany. The trip would include the usual tourist stops, as we would be traveling on tourist visas.

Nigeria was selected as the starting point from which to begin our vacation. To support our tourist status, we visited the local zoo as representatives of a small zoo in California. We stayed for one week in Nigeria and spent most of our time in Lagos and some small villages on the outskirts of the capital. We then traveled from Nigeria to Liberia, which was one of the main goals of our trip.

There were things happening in Liberia that had our government concerned. Liberia had always been a pro-western government until William R. Tolbert became president (1971–1980). Shortly after he took over the presidency, he started establishing strong relationships with the Soviet Union, the People's Republic of China, and Cuba.

The Cold War was raging, and any country that started showing favoritism toward these Cold War enemies was a major concern to our leaders.

The breaking point came when Liberia severed their diplomatic ties with Israel during the Yom Kippur War (1973) and presidentially supported the idea of granting national rights for the Palestinian people. It became obvious to our leaders that we needed to gain more intelligence on Liberia and its intentions before it became a destabilizing force in the area.

We needed to gather the necessary intelligence so that we would be ready to counter any movement by President Tolbert that would shift the balance of power in the region. Our mission was to gather intelligence from the local contacts and look for any sign of Russia's involvement in Liberia.

We landed in Monrovia, Liberia, at the International Airport, which was also the local military base and was strictly controlled by soldiers with automatic rifles. The stewardess had warned all passengers before we disembarked the plane that the soldiers would react very forcibly with anyone caught taking pictures.

While we were on the ground we were forbidden to leave the airport, so the four of us walked around the inside of the terminal, looking at the runways and hangars that were clearly visible from inside. We noticed that there were some Russian Migs and other support aircraft in a remote portion of the airport. Upon seeing the aircraft, we knew we needed to obtain pictures so our intelligence division could evaluate the threat.

The company had supplied us with miniature cameras that they carefully hid in our clothing with the anticipation of such a situation. The question facing us now was how to take the pictures without getting caught by the soldiers who were carefully scrutinizing everyone.

I volunteered to create a distraction that would draw the soldiers away from the windows while one agent covered their backs and the other two took the pictures.

To create a disruption, I entered the men's restroom and went to the "squat potties," as I called them. The squat potties consisted of two footprints that you stood on that were directly over a hole in the floor. You conducted your business in this hole. I started creating a disturbance when the attendant (a lady) came over and stood beside me with toilet paper draped over her arm, waiting for me to finish my business.

I jumped up and started yelling that I wanted her out of the room and that I would hold my own papers, thank you. I started yelling at the soldiers that I wanted privacy and demanded that they remove the woman from the restroom.

When the soldiers learned of my problem, they started laughing at me and mockingly explained to me that I was not in the United States. They said I was in their country, and I would have to do it their way, or I could just wait until I got back on the plane. They were laughing and talking among themselves as they continually pointed at me, and they seemed to get great joy out of sharing my discomfort with anyone who would listen.

I looked over at my partners and saw them walking away from the windows, so I knew they had completed their assignment. I then quieted down, went and sat on a bench, and waited patiently for the order to board the plane.

All the time I was sitting on the bench the soldiers continued to laugh, point at me, and said things to the attendant. Little did they know that the final laugh was on them.

I mentioned the Yom Kippur War of 1973 as the basis of our concern about Liberia, but that war was the reason for this entire trip. The war, also referred to as the Arab-Israel War, started when Egypt and Syria launched a surprise attack on Israel during their most holy day when Israelites were forbidden to fight unless it was in defense. The Arab nations quickly captured the Sinai Peninsula and also the Golan Heights but were able to hold them only for a short period until they were driven back by the Israeli Army.

This war lasted only twenty days, but it almost caused World War III. The Soviet Union supported Egypt, and the United States supported Israel. I believe if this war had lasted any longer, the Soviet Union and the United States would have entered into this conflict, and it would have quickly spread and perhaps involved nuclear weapons.

As recorded in history, this war lasted only twenty days but made the United States aware that the Soviet Union had intentions of spreading communism to the Arab countries. The United States had been ignoring the Arab countries for decades, but now a new interest was stirred up. My team was dispatched to the Mideastern countries specifically to gather intelligence on our Cold War enemies.

After we had obtained the necessary information, we left Liberia and flew to Egypt. Once in Egypt we visited the pyramids, the Sphinx, and the Valley of the Kings. We spent some time in Cairo visiting the Museum and seeing the King Tut display. We visited Cairo looking for any sign of the Soviet Union's presence, but we saw no evidence that they were in Egypt.

Upon our leaving Egypt, it was only a short flight to Amman, Jordan, where we were to spend four days. I had an informant in Amman whom I met in 1971 when I made a trip to Damascus, Syria. In 1971, my Armenian friend in the United States had relatives in Syria, and he arranged for me to meet his family and spend some time with them.

I met his family in Damascus and was surprised to hear that they lived in Beirut, Lebanon. They were in Damascus to promote their family business and to maintain contact with relatives in Syria.

In 1973, just prior to our trip, this family contacted me to let me know that they had expanded their family business to Amman, Jordan. They extended me an invitation to visit them if I was ever in the country.

When I found out that my team was going to be in Amman, I immediately contacted this family and asked if they could assist us while we were in the country. I let them know that we were on vacation and would like to see the sights, and I hoped that this would include the ancient city of Petra.

They immediately made reservations for us to stay at a local hotel on the back streets of Amman in an area not frequented by tourists. They felt this hotel would be safer for us because only the locals used it, and it was owned by an Armenian businessman. He felt that the common tourist hotels would be too dangerous because many Egyptians and Syrians lived in those areas, and they maintained a deep hatred toward the United States because of her support of Israel. This hatred was especially strong right now because the war had only come to a halt nine months before our visit.

My friend, Habib, picked us up at the local airport and drove us to our hotel rooms. The hotel was on a small, narrow back street and was two stories high, constructed entirely with gray stones. The rooms we were assigned to were very small and had two single beds in each room. The owners had placed very thin mattresses on top of sheets of plywood, and these were our beds. These accommodations lacked the comforts we were so used to, but we were not in Amman to be comfortable. They advertised that each room had running water, but the correct description would have been dripping water. We lacked comfort, but the location and isolation were perfect for our mission.

As per our training, whenever we left our rooms we placed things in areas that would make it obvious if someone had entered our rooms and what they did in our rooms while we were gone.

I would take a strand of hair from my head and wrap it around the latch on my suitcase so that no one could search my suitcase without my knowing it. I would also take a matchbook, fold it in half, wrap a string around it, and place it on the inside of the door as I closed it. I would then pull the matchbook up to the door while I closed it and then removed the string. I always left it twelve inches away from the hinges, and even if someone tried to replace it, they would never place it twelve inches away. I could always tell if someone entered our room.

Every day when we returned from our travels, we would check our traps, and every day it was obvious that someone had searched our room and suitcases after we left the hotel. It was my professional opinion that it was the Jordanian Secret Police, who obviously were suspicious of us and were trying to find out if we were really tourists or if there was something more sinister about our trip.

Prior to leaving the United States on our mission, we were instructed to visit the City of Petra. I was to spend some time sitting on the stone walls of the ancient buildings located on the old Roman Road. I was to read a bright red book about Petra that a contact would give me in Amman. The red book would identify me to an informant who would pass me some counterfeit Roman coins that would contain hidden information about the involvement of China in the Kingdom of Jordan.

Our intelligence community was starting to get rumors about China desiring to insert herself in world affairs, and there were many rumors about her involvement in the Mideast as well as in Africa.

China would invest a lot of money in the infrastructure of a specific nation, such as soccer fields, paved roads, and other amenities. However, their main purpose was to insert Chinese businessmen into the local economy. The businessmen would gain a foothold in the local economy, and slowly they would take over the nation, city by city.

China even constructed a paved road that connected the country of Cameroon with Central African Republic (CAR). Previously the only road that connected the two countries was dirt. It was almost impossible to drive on, especially during the monsoon season. The paved road benefited both countries, and through this China gained the trust of both countries. To cement their relationship, China also constructed a state-of-the-art soccer stadium in the city of Bangui, the capital of Central African Republic.

Needless to say, this strategy worked, and China started gaining a strong foothold in the Mideast and Africa.

Our informants in Jordan had information about China, and I was to pick up this information that would be embedded in lead coins and bring it back to the United States.

The coins would be lead so that they would pass the X-ray machines and would obviously be counterfeit so that customs would let them pass the borders.

I was to buy the coins as souvenirs and place them in my luggage as I exited the Kingdom of Jordan.

My team and I entered the city of Petra through the narrow Siq that led to the bank. While my team toured the city, I sat on the wall next to the ancient Roman road and read a book given to me in Amman. It had a bright reddish-orange cover and was easy to spot so my contact would quickly see me and pass the information to me.

I was expecting an adult to approach me. I was totally surprised when a young eight- to nine-year-old Bedouin girl came up to me holding three counterfeit coins and under her breath repeated the prearranged phrase in perfect English. I handed her the thirty American dollars that were the prearranged response, and she gave me the coins and was gone just as quick.

Many tourists purchased these coins in Petra because they were not protected by the Department of Antiquities, as they were crude counterfeits, and so it was very common for tourists to buy them.

After we got back to our hotel and started packing for our trip to Israel, I sequestered the coins in a compartment in my suitcase and prepared for our trip to the border between Israel and Jordan. The main border crossing between these two countries was over the

Allenby Bridge, and the only means of transportation open to us was a public bus.

We boarded the bus and immediately noticed that the only passengers aboard this bus were the four of us. I was not surprised there were only the four of us because it had only been nine months since the war, and there was a lot of tension between these two countries.

I was very anxious to leave Jordan because I did not know what the Secret Police knew, but the fact they searched us every day caused me great concern.

As we approached the Allenby Bridge, I noticed that the bridge crossed over a dry riverbed and that both the Jordanians and the Israelis had placed fortified barricades at their ends of the bridge.

Overlooking the bridge were fortified bunkers manned by soldiers. I counted at least three high-caliber machine guns on the Israeli side and RPGs on the Jordanian side, as well as various smaller caliber machine guns.

I knew the ground was saturated with landmines, and, therefore, the only way to Israel was over the bridge and past the Israeli guards.

We stopped at the Jordanian checkpoint and presented our passports. The guards asked many questions about the purpose of our trip, and we stated that we were just tourists visiting the many historical sites.

They noticed that we had been to Africa, Egypt, and now Jordan, and after asking about some specific sites, they opened the barricade and let us drive onto the bridge.

I was just starting to feel relieved when suddenly the Israelis dropped their barricade, and I heard loud shouting and noticed that all of the Israeli soldiers were running to their machine guns.

The Jordanians responded by dropping their barricades and manning their weapons, and suddenly we were trapped in the middle of the bridge with no place to go, and our lives were hanging in the balance.

I vividly remember the conversation we had at that time. Mario, who was one of our team members, made the following statement: "Do you think the Secret Police found out about our mission?"

Robert turned to me and asked, "Where are the coins?"

I replied, "Hidden in my luggage?"

Robert responded, "Do you think we should hide them on the bus?"

Mario then made this observation: "Did you notice it was the Israelis who dropped the barricade first?"

Our consensus was that no one knew about our mission, but we were still in a very dangerous situation.

We evaluated our situation and even discussed leaving the bus and making a break for the Israeli side, but we realized that they would view us as the enemy and kill us on the spot.

We decided the only course of action we could take was to continue pretending to be tourists and prepare for the worst. We gathered our luggage around us and decided if the shooting started, we would lie down on the floor of the bus, gather our luggage around us, and hope for the best.

We all knew that nothing would stop the machine-gun bullets. If the shooting started, we were all dead men.

We were forced to sit on the bus for over four hours in the hot sun before the Israeli Army finally lifted their barricade, and we were allowed to enter Israel.

We were all relieved when we entered Israel Customs and even more relieved when they spotted the counterfeit coins and only laughed among themselves and made disparaging comments about American tourists. They did not know that I understood their language, and I even laughed inside because they'd missed the items that I was smuggling into the country.

The rest of the trip was uneventful, and we returned to the United States with all of the information that we had been commissioned to get.

MISSION COMPLETED

CHAPTER FIVE
BLACK OP

THE COLD WAR

The end of World War II ushered in a five-decade struggle for superiority referred to historically as the Cold War. We called it the Cold War because they did not fight the Cold War with conventional weapons but fought it in four main areas.

The four main areas of warfare were psychological warfare, propaganda, espionage, and technological superiority.

They conducted the psychological and propaganda warfare on many different levels. One well-known method was Radio Free Europe, where England and America broadcast programs and propaganda that boasted of the benefits of democracy and the evils of communism.

The technological warfare centered on the space race, with both sides determined to reach outer space first. The Russians launched the first intercontinental missile, but the United States quickly surpassed them and placed a man on the moon.

The espionage battle was the dirty side of this Cold War. Both nations developed specialized units that excelled on the covert side of this Cold War. The Russians had the KGB, and the United States had a unit that presently is known as the CIA. Both units had spies, moles, and assassins, and both nations engaged in activities that were secret, politically denied, and usually illegal.

During the Cold War, there were some major confrontations that occurred that could have triggered World War III and most likely would have brought worldwide destruction.

The real first crisis after the Suez Canal was the Berlin Blockade of 1948–49. The Russians placed a blockade around Berlin that stopped all foods, materials, and supplies from reaching the people of Berlin. Russia took this action because England and the United States would not let them dominate Berlin.

As a result of the blockade, England and the United States, along with some other allies, started what became known as the Berlin Airlift. This airlift was where we supplied Berlin with all necessary supplies by air and circumvented the standard methods. Russia finally backed off on their demands, and we averted the crisis.

A similar crisis once again occurred in 1961 when Russia was upset that all of the educated people of Berlin were migrating to the west side of Berlin, and East Berlin was stagnating and losing its creative forces. It should be noted that Russia maintained control over East Berlin, and the allies maintained control over West Berlin. To stop this migration, Russia started building the Berlin Wall and in 1961 blocked the only exit route out of East Berlin and totally stopped the migration to freedom. The Berlin Wall remained until the presidency of Ronald Regan, who was instrumental in demanding the wall come down.

The next great crisis started in 1962, when Russia decided to bring nuclear missiles into Cuba. Russia knew the United States was behind the many attempts to overthrow the Cuban government and thought they could stop the United States if they had nuclear missiles on the island.

It is true that the United States made many attempts to overthrow Castro's government, including the Bay of Pigs disaster, but we were never successful.

President Kennedy knew that he could not allow nuclear missiles that close to the United States borders, so he placed an embargo on Cuba and ordered the navy to stop the Russian ships carrying the nuclear missiles. The world was only seconds away from World War III when Russia backed down and withdrew its ships that carried the nuclear missiles.

Everyone knew about these crises because they were so public, but the public was totally unaware of the many other confrontations that were taking place on a daily basis. The Cold War sort of cooled down after the Cuban Missile Crisis, but it reignited in approximately 1970, and this period became known as the Second Cold War.

All of this action was the result of President Harry S. Truman's Doctrine of Containment, which presented the plan to stop the spread of communism by any means necessary. This plan gave full authority to units such as the CIA to institute policies and engage in such actions as they felt necessary to stem the growth of communism.

It was in the late '60s that espionage became the doctrine of the day. It was during this time that I joined the United States Marine Corps and was then recruited by this "company" for special assignments.

My generation grew up with the belief that communism was the greatest danger we would ever face and that Russia was the main propagator of this doctrine. Teachers taught us that Russia wanted to conquer the world and that her intention was to destroy America, the baton-bearer of democracy. After she destroyed the United States, she would rule the world.

We knew that communism was evil, and democracy was good. We also knew this wasn't a battle between Russia and America; this was an epic battle between good and evil, between God and Satan. In those days, we could refer to God and even give credit to Him for the blessings of America.

Early in elementary school we were taught that Russia possessed the atomic bomb and that we could expect them to use it to further communism. We learned the dangers of a nuclear attack and what we were to do in case of such an attack. We had practical drills in school to prepare for such an event. We were taught to lie next to an interior wall, curl up in a ball and cover our head with both arms. We watched many movies showing the dangers of a nuclear war. I remember one that brought fear every time we saw it. There was a bright flash of light with a large mushroom-type cloud rising out of it, and then a wave of energy that destroyed everything in its path. I often wondered why we were trying to protect ourselves when they told us the nuclear blast would kill everything in its path. If we were close enough to see the flash, then we were close enough that the energy wave would kill us. It didn't really matter what we did.

We were also constantly warned about Russia's diabolical intentions and that we, as patriotic Americans, might be called upon to sacrifice our lives for the freedom of our great nation. Our leaders indoctrinated us with the idea that the greatest act of courage was to give our lives for our country. We were all ready and willing to die for the safety of the United States.

I viewed each crisis through the lens of this indoctrination, and I was ready and willing to serve our great country to defend the freedoms that we hold so dear.

That is why I volunteered for this special assignment and why I was willing to do whatever our country asked of me to preserve this freedom for our next generation. I still hold to this doctrine and belief even as I face death. I do not regret anything that I have done for our country, and if called upon again, I would do the same thing.

One of the last semipublic confrontations occurred when the Soviet Union invaded Afghanistan in 1979. Covert agents planted by the CIA spread rumors and planted false evidence that triggered the Soviet invasion of Afghanistan. Once they had invaded Afghanistan, we began to supply stinger missiles and other advanced weapons to the Freedom Fighters and even sent covert operators into the country to train the resistance movement. The covert operators entered Afghanistan through Pakistan and made the trek on foot through the mountains and passes, being led by the Freedom Fighters.

We wanted Russia to be mired down in their version of Vietnam in a war they could not win. A war of this nature would tie up their resources, and we would be free to operate in the rest of the world. The Russians could not win this war and could not change the hearts of the Afghanis because they were a tribal people. They were not loyal to any central government, and they did not want what the Russians were offering. Throughout the history of Afghanistan, no country had ever been able to conquer these warrior tribes.

We tried everything we could to tie up the resources of the Soviet Union, and we were quite successful for many years. The Soviet Union had a similar goal of tying up the resources of the United States, but the method they used was totally different. The method the Soviet Union wanted to use was to expand the chaos within the United States by quietly supporting the native-born dissident movement. This movement was already creating havoc in American society and was tying up many assets, so the Soviet Union decided to assist the dissidents, who would then tie up more of the assets. To achieve this goal, they prepared subversive agents and sent them to America to quietly join the dissidents and provide logistical expertise that might be missing.

They had plenty of dissident movements to operate within because we had been experiencing civil unrest on many national levels. We had been dealing with the antiwar movement, the antigovernment movement (SDS, BLA, SLA, BP, and others), drug culture (hippies, LSD, Leary's group), and the segregationists. Each of these movements provided fertile ground in which the Russians could plant their operators.

I was unaware of the extent that the Soviet Union had infiltrated these movements until February 1976 when they bombed the Casa Del Sol room at Hearst Castle. Patti Hearst had been kidnaped by the Symbionese Liberation Army (SLA), and rumor had it that since her kidnapping, she had chosen to join this group. Naturally, suspicion for the bombing centered on the Symbionese Liberation Army, but nothing was ever legally proven, and even to this day there have been no arrests for the bombing.

On the day of the bombing, I was in the San Luis Obispo area working with other explosive experts. We were developing the technology necessary to safely breach the safety deposit box doors that lined the walls of the many bank vaults.

Authorities suspected the Black Liberation Army of planting bombs in these rented deposit boxes. Members of the Black Liberation Army would rent one box at two different banks. They would place a bomb in each of the two boxes with the timers set to go off twenty-four hours apart. The terrorist group would let the first bomb detonate, and then they would notify the second bank of a similar device in their vaults. They would provide the box number and the name of the person who rented the box. Once they had proven ownership of the box, they demanded that the bank pays a large ransom before they would surrender the key.

Naturally, the banks would not pay the ransom, so bomb technicians had to find a way to enter the boxes without detonating the explosive devices. We wanted to breach the safety deposit box remotely, but with our present technology this was impossible. To defuse the bombs, a technician had to enter the box by methods that required placing themselves in great danger. We wanted to alleviate as much danger to the technician as possible, so we had to find another method for breaching the doors. Helping develop this technology was the reason we were at San Luis Obispo experimenting with bank vaults donated by the banking industry.

When we received news of the explosion at Hearst Castle, we dispatched a handful of experts to assist in the crime scene investigation and to keep us updated on the status of the investigation. Little did I know at that time how this event would play into my next mission.

Shortly after this bombing I received a call from Col. Black, and I was instructed to meet with other agents at a remote mountain cabin in Montana. I arrived first, and within hours of my arrival, the other three team members and Col. Black arrived.

Col. Black reminded us about the bombing at Hearst Castle and said that we would be dealing with this event. Col. Black briefed us about the ongoing operation that centered on a Russian double agent. He was the handler for a covert team of Russian agents who were operating within the borders of the United States.

The Russian agents were to infiltrate the subversive elements within America's society and create chaos by providing expertise and technical support for the violent acts they were contemplating. These Russian agents were well embedded within American society, and the subversive groups were totally unaware of the Soviet Union's involvement, even though I don't think that would have made a difference.

Many of these groups were supporters of communism and other various forms of socialism and would have welcomed support from Cuba or Russia. They were not patriots of America.

Col. Black reminded us of the bombing at Hearst Castle, and while most of us had assumed that it was the job of homegrown terrorists, he informed us that the bomb maker was a covert Russian agent.

The Russian handler for the covert operations within the subversive groups had turned against Russia and was seeking asylum in the United States. This Russian handler had been apprehended by the CIA and was facing life in prison or even death and rather than face either, he turned against Russia and sought asylum. Many people didn't know it, but this is the way we all played the game. Both the Soviet Union and the United States played by these rules. Before America would consider his case, he had to work as a double agent and provide the names of covert operators who were in America, their missions, and their present locations. If he wanted to save himself, he had to deliver other Soviet agents. He sold out the Soviet Union to save his life. Even though we used him, no one respected him.

The first Russian agent he delivered was the bomb maker who had infiltrated the Symbionese Liberation Army and made the device that they'd used in the Hearst Castle bombing. He told us this group of radicals (SLA) was presently planning more attacks on very public landmarks and, in fact, the Russian agent was presently constructing two additional bombs.

They planned the Hearst Castle bombing as a warning, but these two new bombs would contain far more explosives and shrapnel and were intended to claim many more victims. These violent acts were intended to drive fear deep into the heart of American Society and force us to alter our way of living.

He told us that the trademark of this particular Russian Agent was that he always used "Westclox" watches as timers. He also wired the devices with red and green wires because they were "Christmas Presents" for his enemies. He used Westclox watches because they had plastic faces, and you could easily drill through the plastic because other watches had glass faces, and they would shatter when they were drilled.

He said the Russian handler had also provided the names and addresses of two other Russian agents. These agents were embedded in the Black Power movement, white supremacy groups, and certain outlaw biker gangs who were at war with each other.

Col. Black told us that each agent needed to be eliminated without raising any suspicion of our government's involvement, so we were to make the assassinations look like accidents. He said the "accidents" were of extreme importance because we did not want to make Russia aware that we had identified their agents. We also did not want American society to realize that we were terminating people within the borders of the United States without trials.

Our first target was the sadistic agent who had constructed the device used in the Hearst Castle bombing. The information given to us was that he was building two more devices and that he would utilize them in two months during a Fourth of July celebration. He was going to target the military and police units that were providing security.

He gave us the address of this agent, who was going by the name Johnny. He lived alone in a small residence on a very quiet street in a small suburb of Los Angeles. A six-foot-high wooden fence surrounded the entire backyard. The fence was totally covered front and back with climbing vines. There was an alleyway behind the house that was only two feet wide and was obviously an easement for the electric company because power poles lined the alley.

As the alleyway did not transverse the entire block, there would be very little foot traffic, so there was less chance of us being discovered.

The backyard was totally hidden by a vine-covered fence, and our only view of the backyard was by means of satellite photographs that we ordered through the NRO (National Reconnaissance Office).

The backyard was totally secluded, but we were able to identify a small ten-by-ten wooden shack tucked away in the northwest corner of the lot. There was a large oak tree with the branches covering the top of the building, making it almost impossible to observe activities within.

We asked that NRO take photographs every ten minutes so that we would have a real-time view of the activities in the backyard. The NRO provided those photos three days later. We also drilled a small hole in the wooden vine-covered fence and placed a motion-activated camera with a view of the back of the house and the shack. The vines were so thick that we were able to hide the entire camera in those vines. The vines were so thick that there was no possibility of the camera being discovered.

After viewing NRO's photos and our photos from the hidden camera, we could clearly see Johnny leaving the house and entering the shack with various materials that were obviously part of a bomb. The main thing we saw him take to the shack was two single-latch briefcases almost exactly like the one found at Hearst Castle.

Our team was able to rent a vacant house two residences south of the target and on the same side of the street. This house was important because we needed to use the alleyway to reach the shack and to plant our cameras.

We had a lot of intelligence on our target, but we had to identify his daily patterns to find a point of vulnerability. Everyone is vulnerable to being assassinated, and everyone has a weak point. We just had to find it. Two of our team members started tailing our target whenever he left his home, and Robert and I found a way to enter and observe the action inside the shack.

Late one night we started working on the back fence and found that we could remove a couple of wooden slats, which made the hole large enough for us to fit through. The vines were so thick that they totally covered the hole, and we could enter and exit at our will. We were very careful to place the vines back in their original positions so that Johnny would not become suspicious. He was a highly trained agent who was trained to careful observe everything around him for anything that had changed.

We found the target was addicted to Starbucks coffee, and every afternoon he would drive to the local Starbucks and purchase a caramel latte. The daily coffee was the only habit he had, but it takes only one to eliminate a target.

During one of his latte runs, I entered the backyard, climbed the oak tree and got on the roof of the shack. I drilled a small hole into the roof and placed a camera so that I had a view of his entire work bench. By means of this camera, I was able to see most of the inside. The camera was adjustable to the point that I could see him working on a bomb and could even identify the Westclox timer he was using.

As I watched Johnny construct this bomb, I realized what a highly trained professional he was, and I knew it would take all of the skills I possessed to eliminate him successfully. No one would ever know the adrenaline rush I felt when I realized how good he was. The adrenaline rush could only be compared to a hunter who was stalking a nice buck only to find out it was a trophy buck, a one-of-a-kind.

My competitive nature came out, and I relished the mano-a-mano battle that would take place before I eliminated him.

I obsessed over watching him construct his bomb, and I hovered over the screen that recorded his every move and watched for the slightest opening that he would eventually give me. When I spotted that opening, I would pounce on it and eliminate the prey.

I watched as he placed three sticks of dynamite in the briefcase and then ran the negative wire (green) to the power source but wisely did not connect it. He then did something I thought was brilliant. He wired the latch directly into the circuit so that if anyone opened the latch, it would act like a collapsing circuit and by that detonate the dynamite.

He then cut a very small slit in the back of the briefcase and inserted a two-inch-by-one-quarter-inch piece of clear plastic between two electrical contacts. The plastic prevented the circuit from being completed until he removed it. He wired the Westclox timer into the circuit and then connected the green (negative) wire to the battery, leaving only the red (positive) wire to be connected. Once he connected the red wire, the bomb was completed and ready to be used.

You learn a lot about a person as they construct a bomb. I realized that Johnny was a very sadistic man because he placed a two-second delay switch into the circuit. He placed the two-second delay in the circuit so that whoever opened the briefcase would have time to realize they were about to die, but not enough time to escape.

Johnny had a second pattern he always followed. Whenever he left the shed, he would latch the briefcase but not remove the plastic strip. When he returned, he would look at the plastic strip to make sure it was in place before he opened the case to complete his work.

I don't know why he always closed the briefcase, but this was the opening I needed to eliminate him.

I had located Johnny's fatal flaw, and now he would pay the price.

Johnny looked at his Westclox wristwatch and noticed it was time for his daily trip to Starbucks, so he closed the briefcase and left the shed. The surveillance team followed Johnny to make sure he did not change his routine. He was three blocks away when I made my move.

I exited the safe house, entered the alleyway, and made my way to his backyard. I entered the yard, quickly picked the lock on the shed, and accessed the workbench.

I knew the bomb was unarmed, so I opened the briefcase, removed two sticks of dynamite, and attached the red wire to the battery. The bomb was now ready to go except for the plastic strip in the back.

Prior to closing the briefcase, I wrote a very large note in black letters with only one word on it. The word was "oops." I wanted this sadistic Russian agent to know he was going to die and that he had lost the game. I wanted him to feel the fear, the panic of impending death, and I wanted him to know that he had met a better opponent.

The reason I removed two sticks of dynamite was to prevent any collateral damage. I also removed the two sticks of dynamite to assure that the civilian investigators would have enough evidence to reach the conclusion that he was an amateur bomb maker who had accidently killed himself.

I placed my note inside the briefcase on top of the dynamite and then closed the lid.

To arm the device, I removed the plastic strip. I noticed that Johnny always checked the plastic strip before he opened the case, so I cut the plastic strip short and reinserted It Into the slit. I cut it short enough so that it could not touch the contact points, and then I left the shed.

We notified the surveillance team that our task was completed. They said that he had just purchased a cup of coffee and was now headed back toward his residence.

Johnny did not immediately enter the shack, so we maintained constant surveillance on both cameras and waited for him to enter the shack.

Around midnight, I observed him exit his residence and walk toward the shack. He entered the shack and walked directly to the workbench. Our anticipation was extremely high as he looked over the briefcase to make sure everything was intact, and then he pushed the latch to open it.

The look on his face was priceless as he saw the note and realized that someone had armed the bomb. I expected to see fear on his face, but instead of fear a look of hatred emitted from his eyes, and his mouth formed a word that I will leave unsaid. He then looked at the ceiling, directly into the camera, and then our monitor went black.

We heard a small muffled explosion, so we started packing up after a round of high fives.

The news reports the next day and throughout the entire week identified this victim as the prime suspect in the west-coast bombings. The investigation concluded that he had accidentally detonated the bomb that he was making, thereby killing himself.

Each of the other two Russian agents met a similar fate. The conclusion in each case was they died of premature detonations.

For those who lived during those years, you will remember the various news reports of bombers accidentally killing themselves, but now you know the rest of the story.

Were they really accidents or assassinations?

LSD LABS

The Russians saw the opportunity to stir up more chaos by involving themselves in a deeply embedded drug culture that flourished in the Haight-Ashbury district of San Francisco, California.

The drug culture not only flourished in San Francisco, but it quickly spread throughout the United States. Wherever the drug culture went, it created havoc, and it seemed to unite with the hippie movement. For

94

some unknown reason, the hippie movement had also flourished in San Francisco. Many of the dissidents settled in that area, and their main recreation was "free love"," free drugs" and "freeloading". They were a blight on civilization, and I was totally without sympathy for them and the radical element of subversives that shared drugs with them.

One of their leaders was Dr. Timothy O'Leary, who began experimenting with LSD while doing research with the Harvard Psilocybin Project. Harvard eventually terminated him, but even after termination he promoted the therapeutic possibilities of this deadly drug. He started spreading the "good news" of LSD among the hippies and other dropouts and developed a very large following.

He coined the phrase "turn on, tune in, drop out." This phrase became one of the mottos of the disenfranchised youth of that era. He became a hero to that crowd, and LSD became a staple of the drug and subversive elements of society.

The hallucinatory properties of LSD and the altered state of reality it created resulted in many deaths and injuries to both the users and the innocent victims of the resultant violence. One side effect of LSD that I witnessed firsthand was the mistaken belief that a person could fly.

I was in San Francisco, walking through the Haight-Ashbury District when there was a ruckus just ahead of me. Everyone was looking at the top of a five-story building. When I looked, I saw a person standing on the edge of a flat roof dressed in tie-dyed cotton shirt with Levi pants, sporting an unkempt beard, and waving his arms like he was an eagle. He dove off the roof, waving his arms like they were wings. He maintained this posture until he crashed through an awning in front of a business and landed on a cement advertising sign located in front of the local business.

Needless to say, he could not fly, and his life ended that day the results of a bad trip on LSD.

Elevated body temperature was another side effect of LSD that drove users to seek water to cool down. They would jump into fountains, swimming pools, and lakes in attempts to keep cool. One survivor told me that he jumped into the local swimming pool while on a "trip" and began to see kaleidoscope designs and colors. He so enjoyed the beauty that he decided to stay underwater and enjoy the view.

I asked him about the need to "breathe" the air, and he told me that he knew he could breathe underwater just like a fish, so he just started trying to breathe. He never realized that he was drowning until someone pulled him from the pool and paramedics successfully resuscitated him. This young man was very fortunate; many others were not and died as a result of their drug usage. There were so many young drowning victims that they filled the morgue.

LSD was not the only destructive drug that this culture was using. There was another drug that was even more insidious than LSD. This extremely dangerous drug was PCP. In many cases, the PCP was sprinkled in marijuana cigarettes and was sold on the street under such names as "superweed," "rocket fuel" and other descriptive labels.

Some of the common effects of PCP were that the users became violent, suicidal, severely disoriented, and oblivious to pain. They also had superhuman strength to where I once witnessed a young man under the influence of PCP being arrested. He weighed about 120 pounds and stood maybe five foot three. The eight police officers handcuffed his hands behind his back, and as they were placing him in a police car, he broke the cuffs and began to assault the police officers. They were finally able to get two pairs of handcuffs around his wrists and safely place him in a police car.

I am describing these two drugs because these were the two drugs that the Russians agents decided to utilize as they spread chaos throughout American society. Even without the Russian agents' assistance, these drugs were extracting a tremendous toll on society. The overdoses, violence, psychosis, related mental health problems, injuries, and volumes of court cases were slowly bringing society to a standstill.

The Russians hoped to capitalize on the drug problems, and by exacerbating this drain upon society, they hoped to force America to withdraw from international confrontations and concentrate on stabilizing our society.

The Russians figured if they could get enough drugs into the hands of the disenfranchised youth, then the chaos would increase and would tie up valuable assets. If they tied up these assets, then we could not use them overseas. This plan was insidious, but it would work.

The Russian agents were all university-trained chemists and experts in all kinds of drugs and the manufacturing of these drugs. The plan was for these agents to manufacture high-quality drugs, specifically LSD and PCP, while developing a chain of distributors who would place the drugs in the users' hands.

The drugs were very high quality. The Russian agents sold them to the distributors and users at below market prices. The drugs were sold for less that it cost to produce them, so people began to flock to these manufacturers, not knowing they were Russian agents.

The agents would manufacture top-quality LSD and PCP for two or three months and then they would alter the formula and introduce other chemicals that they knew would invoke unpredictable and often violent behavior in the users.

The Russian handler told us that the agents knew what violent behavior these new chemicals would invoke because they had experimented on the prisoners held in the Siberian prisons for many years.

The file Col. Black handed us on these agents detailed the exact formulas being utilized and the destructive chemicals being introduced on a systematic timetable. This devious plan was working because Col. Black's report also gave the statistics on the national increase in violence, injuries, and deaths caused by these drugs.

The news was always reporting on the violence and deaths attributed to drugs but placed the blame on the chemicals the distributors were using to cut the drugs. They placed the blame on the greed of the drug dealers and never even came close to the real plot behind these two drugs.

Altering these drugs was a covert mission by our Cold War adversary. The reporters were reporting the facts but were unaware of the real story that was taking place. If my team were successful, the reporters would still be blind, even after we eliminated the Russian agents.

The bomb manufacturers were very easy to neutralize. The drug manufacturers proved to be a more complex problem, but we would still do it.

The easy part of this assignment was to neutralize these agents; the difficult part was to make it look like an accident.

Two of us on my team had degrees in chemistry. These degrees allowed us to analyze each step of the manufacturing process and find the point of vulnerability that would allow us to eliminate these agents successfully. With the bombers, we knew the weakness was the electrical circuit and the blasting cap. With the drug-makers, we knew it had to be in the formula and the mixing of the chemicals. Illegal labs were exploding all the time, so we just had to find a way to cause this explosion without being detected.

We analyzed the process over the next week and settled on the idea of covertly switching chemicals on the Russian agents so that they would eliminate themselves during the manufacturing of the drugs.

Through our investigation, we noticed that during the fourth step of the manufacturing process, the manufacturer would add a clear, odorless chemical. They would then put the beaker under a flame to increase the speed of a chemical reaction.

We decided the fourth step was the perfect opportunity to introduce a deadly combination of chemicals without the Russian agents' knowledge, so we spent a couple of weeks working out different possibilities.

We did all of our calculations on papers, so we needed to field test this theory.

Our theory was that the chemical we added would form a gas that when introduced to heat would explode. The explosion would have such force that it would kill the agent immediately, and the evidence would be destroyed in the resultant fire.

The Russian agent we decided to use as a guinea pig was producing LSD in a desert lab south of Lucerne Valley, California. It was a very desolate area, so we could operate with impunity. They were using an abandoned trailer located on a hilltop overlooking a secluded mine shaft, so the substitution was easy to achieve.

The trailer was easy to break into, and the substitution of chemicals was just a matter of exchanging glass bottles. We were in and out of the trailer within minutes. Once we had substituted the explosive chemical, we maintained visual from another mine shaft located on the side of a mountain directly across the street from a cement factory. We were approximately half a mile from the trailer. The trailer was clearly visible from our vantage point even without the use of binoculars.

We waited for approximately three days when suddenly the trailer and the agent disappeared in a fiery ball of chemicals that lit up the entire night sky. I knew the force of the explosion would kill the agent instantly, and the fire would destroy all possible evidence.

The field test was an exceptional success.

FINAL ANALYSIS

We used similar tactics on the rest of the Russian agents, and no one ever suspected the involvement of the intelligence community.

All of the local investigators reached the same conclusion on their investigations. The conclusion they reached was that all of the deaths were the result of accidents caused by carelessness.

The final declaration in each case was that the victim died while participating in criminal activities, and the cases were then closed with no arrests being made.

Society will never know how many of those explosions were accidents or how many were neutralizations, but the overall mission was declared to be a success.

CASE CLOSED. NO ARRESTS. PERPETRATORS DEAD ON ARRIVAL.

CHAPTER SIX
MOTHBALLED

NEW MORALITY
During the time that I had been risking my neck protecting our great nation, society had been slowly evolving into a sanctimonious, left-leaning group of bleeding-hearted liberals. These liberals formed a coalition with the intent of reshaping our American culture.

We didn't need to reshape society; we just needed a group of patriotic Americans who were willing to die to preserve our nation in the form that our founding fathers intended.

Every target I helped eliminate was a threat against the citizens of America. By assassinating these threats, I protected the rights of these left-leaning liberals to pursue the formation of a new society that I distrusted and totally disliked. Little did I know how these liberals would affect my team.

I believe it was on June 13, 1971, when *The New York Times* published the first installment of the "Pentagon Papers". It was through these papers that the public first became aware that governmentally sanctioned assassinations and associated covert missions were taking place.

The government continually lied to the public about the government's involvement in these covert missions, and even when the news reporters got close, they could never link the government with the activities. The public was being lied to by our government, and most of the covert missions carried with them a governmental level of deniability. Every operator knew that if they were arrested by any foreign governments or even our own government, the political officials would deny any involvement. Every operator was aware of and accepted as part of the job the risk of being abandoned by our government. The deniability factor was why we were hired. We were not boy scouts, and we did not pretend to be.

The Pentagon Papers began to unveil the cloak of secrecy over these missions. The Pentagon Papers were the official report by a task force created by Secretary of Defense Robert McNamara. McNamara initiated the investigation and wrote the report without the knowledge of President Lyndon Johnson. Daniel Ellsberg obtained the papers and released them to *The New York Times* after some high-up government officials showed no interest in them.

These papers revealed that our government was using the covert military, CIA, and nonmilitary companies to attack and bomb Cambodia, Laos, and North Vietnam and was involved in many other covert activities including assassinations. Facts proved that our government was aware of and maybe even participated in the assassination of President Ngo Dinh Diem when the Vietnam military coup took place in 1963. These facts were revealed in the Pentagon Papers and provided the first public insight into the inner workings of our clandestine activities.

These facts did not come out until 1971, but it brought into public awareness that our government was participating in covert activities that were never reported to the public. The public reacted with demonstrations, and even Congress responded negatively to this revelation. They could not seem to grasp the idea that our government could participate in or even condone assassinations.

The simple fact is that assassinations have been taking place ever since nations began fighting against nations. We have always targeted officers, especially generals for elimination, and we have also included high-value targets, even if they were civilians.

There was a well-known sniper in Vietnam who spent three days getting into a position whereby he could assassinate an enemy general. He took one shot, eliminated the general, and then managed to evade the enemy and return to his friendly line. The military leaders commended him for his bravery, and no one questioned the validity of the mission because it was war.

In war, the idea is to kill your opponent and to defeat your enemy. The public seemed shocked when they found out that people were dying in a war that did not have a well-defined area called the "front." The enemy could be anywhere, and a good army had the ability to eliminate them even if they were not on the front lines and maybe didn't even carry a gun.

When *The New York Times* made the public aware of the assassinations, it was like a light bulb came on in the minds of the public. The public seemed shocked that assassins existed and that they were part of our national defenses. As a result of the Pentagon Papers, the public found out about the assassinations, and they also assumed that these assassinations were only taking place overseas. No one ever suspected that these activities were also occurring within our borders. I attribute this to the success of my team and others like us.

The response to this revelation from the war-weary demonstrators was instant and sometimes violent. The pressure put on our politicians was tremendous, and it was obvious that our politicians would cave into the pressure and this form of national defense would become obsolete.

This self-fulfilling prophecy came to pass on February 18, 1976, when President Gerald Ford signed Executive Order #11905 that banned "political assassinations." Section 5(g) was entitled "Prohibition of Assassination" and contained the following: "No employee of the United States government shall engage in, or conspire to engage in, political assassination."

This wording pacified the general public, but I was not an employee of the government, and for this reason, this executive order did not even pertain to me or my team. The keywords for the government were "engage in." They could select the target, but only an independent contractor could perform the assassination.

President Jimmy Carter went even further on January 24, 1978, when he even forbade America's involvement in assassinations by signing Executive Order #12036. Section 2–305 of this order stated, "No person employed by or acting on behalf of the United States government shall engage in, or conspire to engage in, assassination."

President Jimmy Carter added the wording "acting on behalf of the United States government." This wording again could easily be overlooked because we were not "acting on behalf" of the government. We were working for an independent contractor and acting for the good of the United States.

President Ford said we could not "do" the assassinations, but did not stop us from being involved (planning). President Carter stopped us from being physically involved in the instrumentation (planning) of the assassinations. President Ronald Reagan put the final nail in the coffin by issuing Executive Order #12333, Part 2.11.

The executive order stated, "No person employed by or acting on behalf of the United States government shall engage in, or conspire to engage in, assassination."

Part 2.11 was the exact wording found in Executive Order #12036, but President Reagan inserted part 2.12 which stated, "Indirect Participation. No agency of the Intelligence Committee shall participate in or request any person to undertake activities forbidden by this order."

President Ronald Reagan closed the final loophole in the executive orders, and at this point, no one was willing to violate these new orders, so Part 2.12 effectively eliminated the mission of my Special Ops team.

In 1985, we were unofficially decommissioned because we never officially existed. We were then, as a team, packed in mothballs and stored in the hidden closet of history.

DECOMMISSIONED

When I received this news, I was rather elated because for over two decades, I had been leading a double life. There was a public me and there was the real me, but I had to separate the two. Even my wife, my children, and my extended family were unaware of what I did when I went to the "business trips" or the "extended training classes."

My wife was only allowed into my public life, and for this reason she was totally unaware of my alter ego. She knew I had been a marine, and she was even aware that I had been accepted into Special Forces, but beyond that she had no inkling. I was able to blame some of my dreams and reflexes on this past training, and she seemed ready to accept this excuse.

I remember one particular night after I had just returned from a mission. I had a very vivid nightmare as I relived a dangerous encounter that had occurred during this mission.

We were both in bed, asleep, when in my dream I was walking down a back alley in a distant third-world country. As I walked down the alley, I was suddenly attacked by an assailant who leaped out of a darkened doorway and tried to kill me with a knife.

In real life, I delivered a karate chop to his throat, snapped his arm, and then stomped on his groin before I turned to defend myself from his partner who started running away. I chased the partner for a short distance before I melted into the dark and made my escape by blending back into the crowds walking along the main thoroughfare.

In my dream, I delivered the karate chop, but instead of it being my opponent, it was my sleeping wife's right leg that had accidently rubbed against me. I was still asleep when I hit my wife, so I continued in my dream and leaped out of bed and started chasing the other man down the hallway. I leaped through the bedroom door and ended up lying on the hallway floor when the man I was fighting suddenly evaporated from view.

By the time I woke up, my wife was screaming in pain and fear. She had no idea what had happened other than she was developing a very large bruise on her right leg, and her peaceful husband was fighting an imaginary assailant in the hallway of our house.

She insisted I turn on every light in the house, and we checked everywhere for the intruder, who naturally was not there. We checked the house together, and when she was fully convinced the house was secure and that it was just a dream I was having, she wanted to know what I was dreaming about.

I quickly concocted a story about having just watched an action movie about war and said that I was just dreaming about one of the scenes. I told her in the movie, someone had attacked the hero, and he had defended himself with a karate blow. I assured her that the dream was the result of the movie, and most likely I would never have another dream of that nature.

I apologized to her, and luckily she accepted both my apology and my concocted story. We went back to bed, but it was months before she would sleep in the dark again. She also insisted that if I chose to watch a war movie, I would spend that night sleeping on the couch in the living room.

I faithfully fulfilled my end of the bargain, and life slowly began to return to normal.

EMOTIONS, A VICTIM OF MURDER

My wife often described me to her friends as a choleric personality, which she described as mostly logic with very few emotions. My mother, on the other hand, described me as a very sensitive child who became hardened through the influence of the Marine Corps.

The truth is that I started out being sensitive, but I quickly stifled my emotions so that I would not be hurt in life. Emotions allow a person to be hurt, and it also makes them vulnerable to feelings.

I could not allow myself the luxury of emotions because emotions could and would cause me to become careless on a mission, and that carelessness could and most likely would result in my or my partner's death.

My job was to kill, and if I had any sympathy for the target or thought of him as a person, then I might be hesitant to deliver a fatal blow. Any hesitation on my part could allow him time to escape or defend himself.

I buried my emotions so deep that for all practical purposes, I was emotionally dead. My emotional void affected my relationship as a husband and as a father, and it left a void in my psyche. When you stop to realize that I also had shut my family out of my "real" life, you begin to envision who I had become.

I operated more like a machine than a loving husband and father, yet deep within myself I wondered what it would be like to experience emotions again. What would it be like to feel love rather than just exist?

Now that I was decommissioned, I wanted to know what emotions felt like again. I wondered if this was possible.

Once your emotions are dead, can they come back to life?

Maybe I was too far gone ever to experience love again.

Maybe, after all the people I had eliminated, I didn't deserve to experience normal emotions.

All of these thoughts were flowing through my mind as I came to grips with the reality of being decommissioned.

NORMALITY

Once my release from my Special Ops team was complete, I sat down with my wife, Sandy, and told her that I wanted to start a new phase in our lives. I would not let work be my top priority anymore.

I said, "I want a new relationship with you and the kids. I want to enjoy whatever life we have left. I know I have been paranoid and obsessed with my work, but I want to learn to relax and enjoy this world around us."

My wife silently looked at me for what seemed like five minutes and then asked, "Are you done with the special assignments?"

I was stunned by her question because I had carefully hidden this side of my life from everyone. My life often depended on my cover story and my ability to live a double life, and I had thought I was very good at it.

I said, "What are you talking about?"

Sandy said, "I have always been aware that you had a dark side. Sometimes I got a glimpse of your dark side, and it scared me, but I knew I was safe."

I once again said, "What are you talking about?" I said this because I did not want to admit to anything that she might still be wondering about. I wasn't ready to open up and admit to missions that were still top secret.

She asked me if I remembered a trip to San Diego when three men pulled up alongside us on a deserted portion of the road and tried to force us off the road. She said it was dark out, and she was afraid of what would happen if they were able to force us off the road.

I did remember the trip, so I asked her what it was about the incident that scared her.

She said, "When you started to pull over, I looked at your face, and fear gripped me. You were totally without emotions, and I could see in your eyes that you were going to kill or hurt the three men."

She said, "I was so relieved when they kept driving, and after that short chase, you let them go."

She said, "There were other occasions when we were in dangerous situations, and that same look came upon your face. Your eyes were devoid of any feelings, and I could sense your muscles tense up as you were ready to spring into action. I knew that violence could erupt at any time, yet I knew that I was safe."

She said, "Do you remember the time we met our friend at a restaurant in Riverside? We were sitting at the table with her when suddenly I saw a man enter the restaurant, and I grabbed your arm and told you my blood ran cold when I saw him?

"You didn't say anything. You just looked at him until he saw you.

"I was shocked and scared when he walked up to our table and greeted you by your nickname.

"When he asked to speak to you and you got up and joined him at a nearby table, I suddenly realized he was the man who had accompanied you to Mexico. You told me it was for immersion training in Spanish.

"I overheard him to ask you if you wanted to join him in another mission somewhere in South America. He said it would be for no longer than six months, and you all had a fifty/fifty chance of returning, but that the money was very good.

"I was totally relieved when you said no.

"I also realized that you were involved in something that I had no concept of, but I knew it was for the good of our country. I determined at that time to not ask any questions, but I would try to enjoy the part of you the kids and I had.

"I started to relax when you told him you retired from that line of work and just wanted to enjoy your life with me and the kids."

I looked at her and quietly acknowledged that her suspicions were right. I was involved in various clandestine activities in the past, but I was now officially retired, and I had finished my final mission.

She asked me, "Will I ever know what you have done?"

I quietly told her no, and she said that she would never ask anything more about them.

I realized that we were now starting a new life, and I determined that I would never hide anything from her again.

For the first time in ages, I was not afraid to release my emotions, and it felt good.

CHAPTER SEVEN
KICKED IN THE TEETH

It has now been twenty years since they decommissioned me, and I have to tell you it has been good.

It took me all of those twenty years to let my guard down, but I still liked to sit with my back against the wall, and I liked to face the door. I didn't know if I would ever overcome these precautions, but I no longer insisted on these arrangements. In fact, my son, who was a police officer, sat with his back against the wall and always faced the door, and I took the most vulnerable position.

I remember the first time my son, our wives, and I entered a restaurant and were escorted to a booth. My son and I both went for the seat against the wall. This left our wives laughing as they sat together on one side of the booth, and my son and I sat on the other side.

As I learned to relax, I also learned to release my emotions. I began to feel and express love and to enjoy my time with my family and friends. My wife still said I experienced emotions internally, and she hoped one day I would learn to express my emotions in a more public manner, but she would enjoy what she had.

From early childhood, I never had been a very emotional person, and I had never liked to show my emotions publically, but at least then I did have emotions.

The love I had for my wife, my children, and my grandchildren was without bounds. I was enjoying life as I felt their love for me also. Those twenty years had been good for me, and I hoped they had been as good for my wife, children, and grandchildren.

Everyone in my family agreed to let the past go, and no one had tried to pry into my past, except for a couple of reporters who thought they had a story. Someone gave them my name and told them to question me about certain events that occurred while I was visiting one specific country as a tourist, but after a short exchange, they left me alone.

I remember the exchange went something like this.

"I heard that you were involved in the operation that took place in ____."

My response was: "I was never there, but if I was there, I was never involved in the incident that you are talking about. There also is no evidence that the incident ever took place, so I have no response to questions about something that most likely never occurred and if it did occur most likely did not involve me."

I politely thanked them for their time, and I excused myself.

This interview was the only time that my past ever came up. That incident with the reporters happened shortly after they decommissioned us. Since then, I had been left alone to enjoy my new life.

I enjoyed everything about my personal life, but I was becoming more and more concerned about American society. There was a new breed of politician in Washington who was embarking on a course of action that I believed would destroy our country as my generation had known it.

They forgot the lessons we learned during the Cold War, and they were embracing Russia as if she was our most trusted comrade. They forgot that Russia's stated goal was to rule the world through the forces of communism.

Our politicians seemed to believe that when the demise of the Soviet Union occurred in 1990, the threat to our country was removed. They didn't seem to realize that while the Soviet Union fell apart, what remained was Russia. Russia still desired to rule the world and was constantly confronting the United States in her fight to support other democratic countries.

One of the main countries that we supported was Israel. Prior to May 14, 1948, we, the United States, supported the establishment of Israel as a sovereign nation, and we had been her greatest supporter since then.

The greatest danger to Israel at that time was Iran. Iran supported the destruction of Israel and had long supported various terrorist organizations that had sworn to destroy Israel. Iran supplied military arms and financial support to terrorist groups that had vowed to destroy Israel. Even though she denied this involvement; the evidence was clear. Iran also had long desired to possess nuclear weapons, and lately they had actively been pursuing that ambition and seemed to be at the point where they would have nuclear capabilities within a couple of years. The United States had made every effort through the United Nations to prevent Iran from obtaining this capability, but all of our efforts had been in vain, mainly because of Russia and to some extent China.

In the United Nations, there were five countries with veto power, referred to as the P5. These countries were China, France, Russia, the United Kingdom, and the United States. Our American politicians didn't seem to realize that Russia and China always vetoed any motion made by the United States, especially concerning Iran and her enrichment of uranium. Russia was heavily invested in Iran and was one of her largest trading partners. China also provided material and other equipment, including centrifuges that were necessary to the enrichment of the uranium. They were not about to confront Iran about Israel when there was so much money at stake.

With these facts in mind, our president still confided with his Russian counterparts. Our president was overheard on a live mic making the following statement: "Let me get reelected first. Then I'll have a better chance of making something happen on these issues, but particularly missile defense, this can be solved, but it's important for him to give me space."

He went on to say, "This is my last election. After my election, I'll have more flexibility."

Russian President Medvedev replied, "I understand."

When I heard this statement, I realized how naïve our president was and how he was acting like he was playing golf with a friend rather than interacting with a representative of a foreign power.

Our president was also overheard talking about our "closest ally in the Mideast," Israel, and his statements about the prime minister of Israel were even more disturbing to me. This conversation was recorded on a live mic also while our president was having a conversation with the French President Nicolas Sarkozy.

Nicolas Sarkozy said, "I can't stand him anymore. He's a liar." He made this statement during a conversation concerning Prime Minister Netanyahu of Israel.

Our president's response was, "You've had enough of him, but I have to deal with him every day!"

It was obvious to me that our president was very intimate with our long-time enemy, Russia, but disliked our long-time ally, Israel.

My concern, maybe even fear, rose to a new level in September 2012 when Prime Minister Netanyahu of Israel spoke at the United Nations. Prime Minister

Netanyahu demanded that the United Nations draw a red line in the sand concerning Iran and her desire to enrich uranium. He showed very clear evidence that by June of 2013, Iran would have enough uranium to construct a nuclear bomb and that Israel would have to destroy the enrichment factories prior to that date. He was asking the world powers to support Israel, but even the president of the United States ignored his plea.

I understood what Netanyahu was saying, but no one seemed to be taking him seriously. When our president went to Las Vegas rather than immediately meet with Prime Minister Netanyahu, I was very concerned because I knew our president was ignoring him also.

I was reading Netanyahu's body language, and he was serious about that date. I believed that the Mideast would be involved in a war during the first part of 2015, and we would either abandon Israel or be involved in World War III.

I was very relieved when Iran revealed that a computer worm had infected all of the centrifuges in Iran and had set their nuclear program back by as much as a couple years. We didn't know how much time this computer worm gained us, but It was not necessary to attack Iran right now.

My life was so good right then, and I didn't want it destroyed, but yet I felt the dark clouds of war gathering on the horizon.

I did not share my premonitions with my wife or children because I did not want to frighten them, and I didn't believe that it would alter anything if I were to share. They were oblivious to the world situation, and perhaps that was a good thing.

I made preparations secretly, and I decided to keep my concerns to myself. These preparations were the first secrets that I had kept since I told my wife about my past, but it was again necessary. I occasionally mentioned my concerns to my wife, but she didn't pursue the topic, so I just let it drop.

I started making secret preparations in case of war and started stockpiling survival equipment and weapons in a metal shed that I had recently purchased. I had enough food, water, and supplies on hand to last my immediate family for three months. I had also located two safe areas where we could flee to, where I could establish a safe perimeter. There was also a fresh supply of water in those locations, and I would be able to obtain some fresh meat and other protein in the case of an emergency.

I may have sounded paranoid, but I would rather spend my time preparing for unknown situations than to trust in luck.

Luck will kill you; preparation will save you.

All the time I was making these preparations I was glued to the television watching news accounts of Iran, Russia, China, and Israel. I was also contacting any intelligence sources that I still had available, and Col. Black had been very generous with his insider information.

I remembered when Iran was one of America's closest and most trusted allies. The relationship changed in 1979 when students overthrew the Shah of Iran, Mohammad Reza Pahlavi, and his dictatorship was replaced by a theocratic regime.

The new regime turned against America and very soon declared Israel to be an illegal occupier of their land. They vowed that they would eliminate Israel from the face of this earth, and they began a campaign within the United Nations to delegitimize their claim to the land.

In the early 1950s, America assisted Iran with the development of their nuclear program by sponsoring the Atoms for Peace project. When Iran turned against America and Israel, we withdrew our support for this program, but Russia, China, and North Korea soon filled the gap.

Russia sent their nuclear scientists to assist Iran, and China, along with North Korea, began to sell them the necessary hardware to enrich the uranium. North Korea sold Iran the missiles necessary to deliver a warhead, and Russia helped modify the missiles so that they could strike targets even in the United States.

Our CIA and Israel's Mossad had irrefutable evidence supporting the accusations that Iran was developing a nuclear bomb. America tried numerous times to place sanctions on Iran, but Russia and China would veto any serious legislation. The United Nations would place minor sanctions on Iran, but within weeks these sanctions would be violated by Russia and China.

Everyone acknowledged that Iran would have nuclear capabilities by the middle of 2013 or at the latest by the start of 2014, but no one would draw a red line in the sand.

Again the computer worm had extended this deadline, but it had not removed the threat. Israel had to make decisions based on the changing world situation, and she could not wait for political changes in the United States to bring the support she needed from the United States.

After being ignored by our president at the United Nations, Israel realized that she would have to defend the Nation of Israel by herself. Israel understood that they were alone in this fight and so they started developing a plan of attack. Col. Black told me that once they agreed to a plan of attack, they set a date for the commencement of the war. Even if Iran agreed to delay their nuclear enrichment program, we must remember that it was only delayed, not stopped. Israel was still going to have to stop the enrichment program, and military action was the only way. Everything else would delay the program, but Israel needed to guarantee that the program was halted, not delayed.

It had been about two months since I last had a conversation with Col. Black, but he called me and told me that Israel had now set a date for the raid. He said the prime minister of Israel, out of a false sense of loyalty to the United States, was going to share the information concerning the attack. He would share it with high-ranking politicians in the United States as well as the president because he knew the immediate repercussions would be great.

Col. Black shared with me that he believed that this false sense of loyalty would endanger the entire mission, and he so advised his counterpart in the Israeli military. Col. Black knew from decades of secret missions how dangerous it was to share top-secret plans with those who had no need to know.

Israel decided to share their plans because they knew that Russia would be furious over the attack. In February of 2015, Russia signed an agreement with Iran whereby she would defend Iran if she were attacked. Russia would also be furious because many Russian scientists would be at the nuclear-enrichment sites, and many would be killed in the initial destructive raid.

I didn't know what would happen when Israel shared their plan with America, but after what I heard our president tell the Russian president about his options after this upcoming election, I was truly worried.

I was truly worried on that Sunday morning as I was waiting for the football game between the Chargers and the 49ers to start. My wife went to church that morning, and I chose to stay at home, relax, and watch some football games.

I was very restless on that Sunday morning. I tried to watch football, but I could not seem to get my mind on the game. After my wife came home from church and noticed by restlessness, she asked me, "What's wrong?"

I told her, "I don't know. Something just isn't right."

She handed me some lunch and said, "Maybe a good lunch will help."

We sat at the table on the porch and started eating together. She told me how much she enjoyed church that morning and then said, "I wish you would join me at church more often. It makes me feel so good when you are with me."

I could see her desire, and I determined to join her, not because I believed in God but because it would make her happy. I told her that I would start going to church with her more, and I instantly saw the pleased look on her face. She kissed me just before she took the plate away and asked if I wanted anything else to munch on during the game.

I said no and then focused my attention on the game.

The 49ers receiver made it to the twenty-four yard line when a Chargers special team member hit him. He hit him with such force that he fumbled the ball, and it started rolling on the ground, as both teams tried to recover it.

I was shouting for the Chargers when suddenly the game was interrupted by a news alert. The broadcaster said, "There is breaking news just coming in from the

Mideast. Our sources are reporting numerous armies have suddenly invaded Israel, and battles are presently taking place as the invading armies seem to be trying to establish control of the mountaintops all over Israel."

He further stated, "Keep your television on this channel, and we will interrupt the game as soon as any further information is available."

The television then went back to the game, and I was left to contemplate the ramifications of this news.

My wife finished the dishes and noticed how intense I was. She asked, "What's wrong?"

I said, "The game was interrupted to announce that Israel is being invaded."

She got very quiet and asked, "What does all this mean?"

I somberly looked at her and said, "We are on the verge of a nuclear holocaust. This world and our lives as we now know them will forever be changed, and I don't know if this world can survive this crisis."

I was not sure she grasped the severity of this situation because she just smiled at me and calmly said, "It's going to be all right. Don't worry."

My cell phone rang, and Col. Black was on the line. He asked me, "Are you watching the news?"

I said, "The news alert came on and reported an invasion of Israel but has now returned to the game."

He calmly said, "Keep tuned. They are right now establishing satellite connections and the picture will be available very soon."

I asked him, "What is happening, and who is attacking Israel?"

He said, "The armies seem to be coming from hidden bases all over the Mideast, and it appears as if Russia is leading the attack. The armies had to be staged already because there was no time for preparation, and the armies suddenly appeared from hidden military bases all over the Mideast."

He further stated, "It was like a hoard of locusts suddenly descended on the mountaintops all over Israel. The invasion was like hundreds of thousands of paratroopers leaped out of planes and battalions of helicopters landed troops and equipment on every mountaintop in Israel."

I asked him, "What caused this attack? We were expecting Israel to precipitate an attack."

He said that Israel's prime minister had a meeting with our president and the State Department and informed them that in two days Israel would launch an attack on the nuclear sites in Iran.

The prime minister of Israel stated, "The attack will only last a couple of days, as the nuclear-enrichment facilities and some infrastructure are our only targets.

"We are not trying to invade Iran, just destroy their ability to enrich uranium and the infrastructure that will allow them to retaliate. As soon as we can do that, we will withdraw and return to our bases."

The prime minister said, "We will keep you apprised of the situation and inform you of the launch of our missiles."

The president responded, "We oppose the attack, and we believe that we can still achieve a peaceful solution through diplomacy."

The prime minister interrupted our president and said, "All you do is talk. We must now act to save our country because they have enriched the uranium."

With that statement, the prime minister ended the conversation.

What Col. Black said next shook my faith in our politicians even more. I always believed that they were naïve, but now I realized they had an ulterior motive, and they would do anything to achieve their goals.

He said, "After the prime minister left the president, he and the head of the State Department placed a call to the leader of Russia and informed him of the pending attack on Iran."

They later claimed that their purpose in revealing the pending attack was to allow Russia time to extract their scientists before the attack, but there was too much evidence that their motives were far more sinister.

Col. Black said, "From all the intelligence we can gather, it appeared as if Russia has been collaborating with Iran and the other Mideast nations. They had been preparing to attack Israel for a couple of years now, so when the president informed Russia of Israel's intent to destroy the enrichment facilities, they decided to attack first."

Russia launched their attack at 4:00 a.m. on the Jewish Sabbath, believing that Israel would be unprepared. The troops launched their attack from hidden bases in Libya, Ethiopia, Egypt, Iran, Iraq, Syria, and Russia, and it was obvious that this plan had been in the process for many years.

I knew our politicians were naïve, but this was no accident. The anti-Israeli sentiment that our government had been showing over the past few years convinced me that our government acted with intent and an ulterior motive.

Col. Black told me that when Russia launched the attack, thousands of helicopters, transport planes, and airborne troops took off from the hidden military bases. It appeared to the Bedouins who observed this as if they had released a plague of locusts that invaded Israel.

Before Israel could even activate their military units, these invading armies controlled all of the high places in Israel, and their missiles were aimed at Jerusalem and every other large city in the land.

The future of Israel was now hanging in the balance. One false move, and the coalition would annihilate Israel.

Our leaders claimed to have been totally caught by surprise, and the official position was that we (America) were totally unaware of the hidden bases spread throughout the Arab nations. Our leaders were saying that since the uprising named the Arab Spring, the United States had lost all of our historical sources of intelligence in the Mideast. The lack of intelligence had made us vulnerable to covert actions such as this.

Our government was blaming everything on the Arab Spring and taking no personal responsibility for having told Russia what Israel was planning.

The "surprise" attack by Russia and her allies left Israel without any local support but the few ships we had in the area. If our government chose to come to the aid of Israel, they could create a diversion by using the firepower on those ships. By creating a diversion, we could buy Israel some time during which we could activate some quick-response units and perhaps save Israel. Based on the record of our government so far, they didn't want to assist Israel, and they wouldn't endanger their political careers by involving us in another war in the Mideast.

I suspended all my other activities, and I stayed glued to my television and my cell phone so that I was in constant contact with Col. Black and my other team members.

Col. Black told me that the president was refusing to send troops or fire any missiles in support of Israel until the United Nations convened and requested such assistances. Hesitation was ludicrous on our part because Israel could not survive that long, and I didn't believe that the United Nations would request such support because China and Russia still had veto powers.

As I was watching the news, I was also able to connect to live satellite, and I could see in real time the mountaintops. I could also see the troops ready to descend on the large cities.

I knew that they were going to attack immediately, and I was sitting in dread because of the many friends I had in Mossad and the Nation of Israel. I had not been able to contact any of them, but I feared for their safety because they would fight to the death rather than surrender.

The only solution I could see was for Israel to unleash her nuclear weapons. I didn't know what would happen to Israel if they did go nuclear, but I also didn't see where they had any other choice. They would be annihilated along with Russia and the Arab nations, but suicide would be better than surrendering to these nations.

I was sitting there pondering Israel's situation, looking at my television screen, when suddenly my television screen produced an extremely bright flash of light that wiped out the picture on my screen.

My screen just went totally red, and then it slowly turned to a smoky gray/black color. I was jolted back to reality as I believed a nuclear war had just started.

God help us and help Israel!

I didn't know what to tell my wife, but I thought I probably should call the kids and warn them about what might happen.

I wanted to have my kids and grandkids here with Sandy and me because maybe I could protect them.

I yelled, "Sandy," and she quickly came to the living room where I was watching the news.

She calmly said, "What is it you want?"

I said, "A nuclear war has just started in Israel, and I want to get the kids here so that we can all be together."

I said, "Look at the television."

She said, "The picture is fuzzy, but it is starting to clear up."

As I looked back at the television, I could see that the picture was starting to come back. Instead of the destruction I expected from a nuclear blast, all I could see were flames on every mountaintop and what appeared to be a trail of flames leading back toward Russia.

I quickly went to Google Maps, and I believed all of the troops on the mountaintops were destroyed. In addition to the troops being destroyed, most of Russia was also in flames.

I was trying to absorb what I was seeing, but I couldn't come up with a feasible explanation for this phenomenon I was seeing. I was totally speechless.

I could see the damage to the mountaintops, but there was no weapon I was familiar with that could cause this kind of damage. The strange part was the damage was visible but only on the mountaintops. Israel was encamped in the valleys, and these were totally untouched.

Col. Black and the rest of my team were as befuddled as I was. None of us had ever seen such a weapon, and one of our team members jokingly said, "It must be an act of God."

My wife had asked me on a couple of occasions, "Why are you so consumed with the Mideast?"

I had to admit, the events that were taking place in the Mideast consumed me, and I firmly believed that a nuclear war was on the horizon. When this phenomenon destroyed Russia and her allies, I knew the threat of nuclear war was alleviated, but I still could not relax. Something kept telling me that something was just not right. I could not put my finger on it, but I had a premonition that something bad was about to happen.

Those many years of living on the edge of danger and death had sharpened my senses, and I was alive today because I learned to listen to those sixth senses.

I could not relax. I was on edge all the time, and I continually walked around the outside of our house, watching the shadows and listening to the sounds of our neighborhood. Every neighborhood produces unique sounds that you can learn if you will take the time to listen. When you learn the sounds of your neighborhood, you will be aware of pending danger because the sounds will change. The change may be very subtle, but subconsciously you will be aware of the change.

How you react to these subtle changes will often determine whether you live or die.

My wife noticed my unrest or "lack of peace," as she referred to it.

Once again, she told me, "Don't worry. Everything is under His control."

I assumed that she was referring to our president, but in my opinion she could never be further from the truth. Our president had a hidden agenda that had directed his every action since he entered the White House. Every president has had their special agendas, but this president's agenda seemed more radical than the others.

Either way, I didn't trust him, and I didn't believe he had everything under control. However, my premonition of danger had nothing to do with the president or anyone else in Washington.

I was not sleeping very well at night. I found myself pacing the floor most of the night, and I often fell asleep from pure exhaustion rather than a desire to sleep.

I think I must have been dozing because I suddenly woke up to a loud sound that was shaking our house. I didn't know if our house was shaking or if it was the vibration of the noise, but I felt the sound waves.

The only way I could describe the noise I was hearing was it sounded like a pack of trumpets all blowing the same note through gigantic speakers all positioned two feet from my ears. The noise was accompanied by a battalion of marines shouting as they charge the enemy, followed by a tornado roaring through my living room, being chased by a locomotive blasting its horns.

The sound was so deafening and powerful that it knocked me to the floor as I tried to get up from my chair. I remembered how we used to throw percussion grenades into the room just prior to breaching the door and the effect the percussion grenade had on everyone who was in that room. Everyone in that room was rendered helpless, and no one ever offered resistance because everything happened so quickly.

Right then, I felt like the inhabitant of that room. I was trying to regain my senses and figure out what happened. As I slowly regained my senses and began to take stock of the situation, dread gripped me because I knew this was no ordinary event. Something just happened that did not fit any scenario that I was ever trained to handle.

We just had a situation with Russia and Israel that went far beyond any one's understanding, and we were still trying to figure out what destroyed Russia and her allies, and then this.

I knew this was the event that I had been trying to figure out, and now we needed to survive until this scenario played out. Whatever was happening was beyond my control, and if we could just survive, then I could make a plan of action.

We would survive!

Everything was quiet, so I yelled, "Sandy," but she did not reply.

I even yelled, "Lulu." That is our dog, but I didn't even hear a bark.

Lulu always barked when something startled her, and Sandy always screamed, but when I looked back, neither one of them ever made a sound.

I searched through the entire house. I searched every room, both downstairs and upstairs, for Sandy or Lulu, but I could not find them anywhere. I ran to the "safe room" that I had built into the house after my last mission, but Sandy and Lulu were not there either. The doors and windows were all secured, but somehow they were missing.

The safe room was where Sandy would have gone because we were both trained to go there in case of emergency. We hid the safe room behind a built-in bookcase that was on the north wall in the downstairs study. I equipped it with weapons, food, and water. These supplies were above and beyond what I had hidden in a storage shed in the parking lot. The walls of the safe room were reinforced, and the entry was almost impenetrable. I built this room specifically to provide safety from intruders, and Sandy would have gone there if she would have had time. I looked all over for her, but I could not find her.

I did not understand what had just happened.

I heard a lot of screaming and other chaos outside my home, but I didn't care what was going on outside. I knew my wife was gone. I didn't know where she went, but I knew I had lost her.

In desperation, I tried calling my kids, but no one would answer their phone. I even called my grandkids and other family members, but all of their phones went unanswered also.

Something catastrophic had once again happened, and I couldn't do anything to protect my family. I had a premonition, but I could not figure it out in time to protect my family. I spent a lifetime protecting my country, but I couldn't even protect my wife. My entire family was wiped out, and I was totally helpless.

I had a premonition that something was going to happen.

I should have been prepared.

When the most important situation in my life arose, I failed.

I let my entire family down.

They were all dead because of me.

That day was probably the darkest day in my entire life. The depth of depression I felt could never adequately be described.

I remember one time during a special training school they placed me in a small box-like structure that removed me from any sensory stimulation. The inside of the box was totally void of any light. It was the darkest dark I had ever experienced. There was no depth perception, and once I tried to scratch my nose and ended up hitting myself in the face.

The inside of the box was totally soundproof, and the box was completely immobilized. Without any sensory stimulation, seconds turned into hours, and days turned into weeks, and your mind began to be your worst enemy.

The depth of darkness I felt sitting in my chair after losing my wife and family can only be understood by those who have spent time in that box.

Darkness and depression engulfed me, and I didn't even care.

I hoped death would find me and end my misery, but all I heard was the phone ringing and ringing and ringing.

I looked at the phone to see if it was my wife or my kids, but it was only Col. Black.

I didn't feel like talking to him, so I just let the phone ring.

For almost one week I just sat in the chair and looked at the walls.

Col. Black just wouldn't give up. He called at least thirty times a day. Finally I gave up and answered the phone.

Col. Black said, "I was hoping that you had survived this last disaster. All the other team members did too."

"I survived, but my entire family is missing, and I have no idea what happened."

Col. Black could tell I was depressed, and I remembered him saying, "You need to gain control of your emotions. Our country needs you, and we need you mentally fit for duty."

He further said, "There are millions of other people missing besides your wife and kids. Every country and nation have been affected with the exceptions of North

Korea and what remains of Iran and Russia. Those three nations claimed that all of their citizens are accounted for and safe."

I asked, "What happened?"

Col. Black said, "The official explanation is that when Russia was destroyed, there was some unknown chemical or biological agent released that quickly spread throughout the entire world, wreaking havoc wherever it blew.

"Some politicians claimed that it was aliens from another universe that attacked us, and they used a chemical agent unknown on this planet. This story shook up many people who were already consumed with UFO conspiracies, but no one took these politicians seriously."

He further stated, "The United Nations explained that the specific chemical released when Russia was destroyed only affected certain DNA types, and only those with certain genetic markers were affected. That was why two people could have been walking together, and only one disappeared."

He then said, "That was probably what happened to your family. They possessed the DNA that was affected by the chemical."

The United Nations went on to explain that no one disappeared. It only seemed that way because the chemicals caused the bodies to self-destruct, and they dissolved the bodies from the inside out. Therefore they only appeared to disappear.

The explanation made sense because we had just come through a few years where people seemed to experience spontaneous combustion. For no apparent reason, they caught fire internally, and we recovered only small parts of their bodies.

It was not a far reach from spontaneous combustion to dissolving internally from reaction to unknown chemicals.

I asked Col. Black if that sounded like a plausible explanation to him, and he stated, "No. I don't believe it, but I have no evidence to the contrary."

I told Col. Black about my safe room and about the cameras and video recorders I had installed around my house. The videotapes would record for twelve hours before they would erase and start over. After my wife disappeared, I immediately reviewed those tapes and was able to view what had happened both at my house and on the streets and freeway around my place.

I told Col. Black that I saw my wife in the kitchen near the oven, and in the next frame she was gone. I told him it was the same with some people in front of my house. One moment they were there, and the next they were gone. I told him that it was instantaneous, and there was no way they disintegrated from the inside out.

He said he had received other reports stating the same thing, but again, the official report was they self-destructed.

Col. Black said, "Regardless of their story, they have asked me to activate our team unofficially so that we can be ready for anything that happens." Officials told Col. Black that everyone in power was also expecting more to happen.

He ended the conversation by saying that he would get me a satellite communication device so that I could monitor world events. I could also listen in to secure lines, and I was to become aware of all situations that were happening in the world.

A short time later, a team member stopped by to give me my phone. I immediately begin to monitor the airwaves.

CHAPTER EIGHT
NEW MAN ON THE BLOCK

PERSONAL THOUGHTS

During my last conversation with Col. Black, he told me to get hold of my emotions because there was a job to do. I tried doing what Col. Black said because I knew he was right. I tried to put my emotions aside, and I did that by concentrating on preparing myself for any mission that might be assigned to us. I was constantly monitoring the radio he gave me, and I was keeping a detailed log of all pertinent data. I needed to be fully informed about every situation I could monitor, regardless of how mundane the information was.

I was gleaning a lot of insight as to how the world was coping with the two disasters that had recently taken place. The destruction of Russia and all of her allies and the subsequent disappearance of millions of people had thrown the entire world into a tailspin. It was approximately two months after those disasters took place, and I was starting to hear conversations that indicated to me that people and nations were slowly recovering, both physically and emotionally. While a slow recovery seems to be in the process, the world was not returning to the status quo that existed prior to the disasters. The innocence or naivety that the world had back then was replaced with a spirit of distrust.

None of the explanations the United Nations gave seems transparent, and no one believed those explanations anyway. No one openly questioned those explanations because there was no other more believable theory being put forward. This scenario caused everyone to distrust everyone else, and I was afraid that this distrust between nations would breed more small wars, which history proved happened.

I used the words "slow recovery," and this was the official word used by the politicians, but I can tell you personally that I had a rough time. So much of my childhood was spent in isolation, separated from "normal" people by life circumstances, that I experienced a lot of loneliness. My deafness separated me from those blessed with the ability to hear. My education separated me from my schoolmates by age and by social ineptness. My military time was spent in isolation, unable to share my missions, even with my closest family members. Now I was once again isolated by world events and the loss of my entire family. Depression and loneliness tried to engulf me at times, and I was trying to cope with the loss of those near and dear to me by submerging myself in my mission.

I was just starting to enjoy the rewards of emotions with my family. I didn't want to return to the emotionally dead person I was before I left Special Ops, but I didn't see where I had a choice. Once again, life had dealt me a twisted hand, and I had no choice but to play it.

It was like there were two people inside of my head. One person didn't want to return to the dark world of isolation, yet the other person said it was necessary to survival. They reactivated me, and so I must once again kill all emotions and rely totally on logic if I was to survive and assist Col. Black.

I knew this was a reality, and I did it, but only out of loyalty to Col. Black and my team. I once again chose to become a machine rather than a human being.

If I had my family to hold on to, I would never have agreed to be reactivated. I would have refused, and I would have clung to my wife, kids, and grandkids and never let go again. The truth is I failed my family, so I didn't have the right to enjoy the emotions and fulfillment that I enjoyed for that short time. You cannot and should not reward failure; I failed, so I deserved whatever came my way.

As I was fighting my personal battle, I was still listening to my communication device because I already knew the outcome of my personal battle. I had nothing to gain by refusing the activation, and maybe this mission would take my mind off my problems and even give me some answers as to what happened to my wife and kids.

Logic dictated my decision, and I knew I would fulfill the mission I was assigned to. I would complete it to the best of my abilities. I would once again put off all of my emotional attachments for logic. I knew I would never see my wife or kids again so, let's just do it.

I would not speak of my emotions or my losses again.

CONFLICTS

As I listened to the communications, I heard that the world leaders were all proclaiming that they had everything under control and that we were entering a period of worldwide peace. They were obviously lying in an attempt to pacify everyone so that everyone would remain calm and cause no problems. As I listened to the worldwide communications, I could see that the opposite scenario was taking place. Things were not in control; in fact, they were spiraling out of control.

There were many areas of conflict that I heard about. Nations were rising against nations, tribes were fighting other tribes, and even families were fighting within themselves. The world leaders were seeking a solution, but as I listened to them, they were unable to either identify the problem or find a solution.

The main area of conflict that I heard about seemed to be a verbal conflict between North and South Korea. They had always had verbal conflicts, but this one was centering on the latest disaster, the missing people. South Korea reported that thousands of its citizens were missing, while North Korea claimed that they could account for all of their citizens.

North Korea had a long history of kidnapping both South Korean and Japanese citizens. These kidnappings occurred both during and immediately after the Korean Conflict. North Korea had a habit of kidnapping scientists, teachers, and other academics because they needed them to resupply their intelligentsia who they lost during the war. The quickest way to do this was to kidnap them and force them to comply with their captors.

During the Korean War (June 25, 1950, to July 25, 1953) there were somewhere in the neighborhood of eighty-four thousand people abducted from South Korea. They were never heard from again. South Korea immediately blamed North Korea, but North Korea denied any involvement, and with no evidence to confront North Korea, the world's superpowers let the issue drop.

After they signed the armistice in 1953, North Korea continued with their program of abductions, and over three thousand more South Korean citizens disappeared. Japan also experienced the treachery of North Korea, as their citizens continued to disappear even as late as 1983. North Korea finally admitted to kidnapping some of Japan's citizens and even allowed some of them to return to Japan as late as the 2000s.

Aware of this history, I was not surprised to overhear the accusations against North Korea, and I believed South Korea was justified in confronting their arch enemy. South Korea once again took their complaint to the United Nations, but once again the United Nations quickly rebuffed them and dismissed their complaint.

The United Nations explained their lack of action by stating, "This problem of missing persons is a worldwide problem, not just a Korean problem."

South Korea was not satisfied with this answer, so they called up their military and began to stage them on the 38th parallel in preparation for an invasion. North Korea responded by moving more of their troops to the 38th parallel, and as has happened so often in the past, we had another armed standoff. The 38th parallel was the imaginary line drawn between North and South Korea when they signed the armistice in 1953.

A replica of this exact standoff had taken place numerous times since 1953, but this time something was different. I remembered when a similar standoff took place in the early 1970s when North Korea crossed over the 38th parallel and killed a few South Koreans who were trimming trees near the demarcation line. There was a lot of tension at that time, but as I said, this time there was something different. There was an unsettledness because of the worldwide turmoil, and South Korea seemed determined to end their conflict with North Korea at this time. I believed South Korea would invade North Korea, and I firmly believed that we were on the brink of another nuclear war.

With so many nations possessing nuclear weapons, it seemed like a nuclear holocaust was just around the corner. First it was Israel and the Muslim countries, and then it was North and South Korea. One mistake, and the world as we knew it would cease to exist.

The countries had been locked in a stalemate for two days. It looked like this might be another case of international posturing rather than a serious confrontation, but the next few days would reveal the truth.

I was still wondering what these two countries were going to do when the silence was shattered one cold Monday morning by the alarm on my cell phone. When I answered it, Col. Black just said, "South Korea has just attacked the North. Start monitoring the radio, and I will get back to you."

I immediately started monitoring that frequency and taking detailed notes.

From what I had previously gleaned, South Korea was positive that North Korea was responsible for her citizens disappearing and decided that they had only one course of action, and that was to attack. They felt they were compelled to take this drastic action, especially after the United Nations said they had no interest in getting involved.

South Korea launched their invasion and immediately made headway against the North Korean Army. Within two days, they had advanced approximately twenty miles into the North, and the North Korean Army was in full retreat.

The whole world, including the United Nations, was riveted on this war. Everyone knew that both nations possess nuclear weapons, and we were fairly certain that the North would use them. I was trying my hardest to decipher what was happening, but with all the confusion that accompanies war, all I heard was garbled communication on the radio traffic. Many people refer to this as the "fog of war." Everyone was talking at one time, and with the limited channels still available, meaningful intelligence was fleeting.

I heard the North Korean field commander credulously report that one of their drones had spotted a lone intruder walking on a frozen part of the Imjin River that flowed between South and North Korea. They didn't know if this was a North Korean trying to infiltrate the South or a South Korean trying to enter the North, but the situation concerned both nations. Walking on the river that runs between two nations at war was very bizarre behavior for any individual, regardless of what his intentions might be. South Korea had just entered the conversation and had ordered the unit closest to the river to converge on him and determine the threat level.

I was totally flabbergasted by the reaction of both nations to this one man. Hundreds of thousands of troops were engaged in battle, and everything seemed to come to a standstill all because of the behavior of this one man.

The North Korean field commander sent troops to capture this man, and I could hear the field commander coordinating his troops in their efforts to capture this invader. The South Korean commander had just ordered his troops to stand back because they were certain that this solitary man was not a danger to their nation. They also wanted to watch and see what North Korea was going to do.

The North Koreans had this man surrounded, but they were just waiting to see what he was going to do. It is almost as if the entire North Korean Army was afraid of this one man. The man was not trying to escape or hide. In fact, he had just sat down on a rock near the river's edge and had extended his hand out toward the North Korean troops. The commander ordered his troops to take this man into custody, and they announced that they captured him.

The actions of this one man were the most bizarre actions I had ever witnessed. Two nations were at war, and because of one man, both nations stopped fighting.

Taking a break because of the actions of one man during a war was something movies were made off, but it was not reality. I would not believe it if I did not hear this with my own ears.

Shortly after they notified their commander that this man was captured, all communication from that area went dead. There was absolute silence, not just from North Korea, but from South Korea also. All attempts to reestablish contact with those troops failed, and for the next three days we heard absolutely nothing from that area. We went from the fog of war to the deathly silence in less than five minutes.

Later I found out that the North Korean secret police took this man from the military and interrogated him for three days. They interrogated this man in an attempt to extract a confession or details of his mission, but for those three days he refused to say a word. The secret police admitted that they had tortured him, beat him, and even waterboarded him, but he never uttered a sound. After the three days of interrogation, the secret police took him before the military tribunal, and it was there that he started talking.

The supreme leader of North Korea stated that at first he just looked each one of them in the eyes and then took a piece of chalk and wrote something on the floor near his feet. They all attempted to read what he had written, but it was in a language that no one understood. He then slowly began to talk in a very quiet and soothing voice, and it was like a supernatural spell came over them, and peace fell over the entire room. No one could remember what he said, but the effects on these battle-hardened soldiers and leaders were indisputable. They said, "It was like a supernatural force grabbed each one of us, and we felt compelled to obey his every command."

The results of that meeting were that the supreme leader of North Korea personally contacted the president of the Republic of Korea (South Korea) and requested a meeting. This meeting was not between high-level representatives, but it was between the leaders themselves. The president of the Republic of Korea agreed to the meeting and soon he found himself face to face with the "invader." He was instantly captivated by the same supernatural spirit of peace.

The end result of this meeting was that both nations agreed to stop hostilities and to begin the transformation into one United Korea under the mentorship of the "invader."

The "miracle" this man performed in bringing the two Koreas to the peace table and even uniting them in peace brought instant fame to this unknown man, only known as "the invader." The United Nations instantly took notice of this man and requested that he become a representative of the United Nations to help broker peace in all of the troubled spots of the world. This young man accepted the position and was formally introduced to the world by the title of Ambassador of World Peace.

When I referred to this man as "young," I was not exaggerating. He appeared to be approximately thirty years of age, but he seemed to possess the wisdom of the ages. Over the next six months, the United Nations sent him to many troubled spots throughout the world, and each time he quickly brokered peace. His successes elevated him almost to the level of a demigod. The world leaders, especially in Europe, what remains of the Mideast, and the United Nations put their trust in his abilities and granted him almost unlimited power.

Shortly after his first six months, this young man addressed the United Nations on the topic of the outdated and ineffective use of the "peacekeeping" forces presently deployed by the United Nations.

He cited statistics from Sudan, the Democratic Republic of the Congo, and Angola to show that the peacekeeping forces were actually responsible for many of the atrocities. These atrocities included rape and murder, and the peacekeeping forces were totally ineffective in fighting the rebel armies in these countries.

He purposed that the United Nations disband all peacekeeping forces and establish a New World Police Force. The New World Police Force would have the power to enforce all laws throughout the world and would also have authority over all local military units and national police forces. This authority would include the FBI, Mossad, KGB, and any other national enforcement bodies, regardless of the nations involved.

He purposed that the World Police Force be placed under his department. It made sense that if he was the Ambassador of World Peace, he needed the ability to enforce world peace, and this new department would be established just for this purpose.

The United Nations placed his proposal on the agenda and said that they would take it up in the next official session.

WORLD POLICE FORCE

The concept of a World Police Force quickly gained acceptance especially in the European countries, and it appeared to me as if the motion to establish a World Police Force would pass with little opposition.

France and Italy became the most vocal nations in support of the Ambassador of World Peace and his concept of a World Police Force. These two nations championed his cause wherever they could.

What surprised me the most and likely sealed his success was the verbal backing given to him by the Vatican. It was not the pope himself who supported the Ambassador of World Peace, but it was his successors. The Pope was one of those who had disappeared with the millions of others, but his position was quickly taken over by powerful cardinals from the European Nations. These cardinals formed an alliance with all other church leaders to help fill the void caused by the disappearance of so many recognized church leaders. They knew they had to be forces for peace and unity if they wanted to continue in their ministries.

The reason they supported the Ambassador of World Peace and the establishment of the World Police Force was because they knew their congregants were stronger when there was an era of peace.

What surprised me was that when the Pope disappeared, so did many other world church leaders. There was no set pattern that determined which church leaders disappeared. Some well-known church leaders were gone, and other very famous church leaders remained. I guess it was more dependent on their DNA rather than their faith or beliefs.

The remaining church leaders formed an association that included all religions and beliefs, including those who had been fighting each other for so many decades. It seemed that the tragedy had finally brought peace between the "men of God."

The powerful church leaders all got together to discuss how they could maintain their control over their congregants and in light of what had happened they decided that they needed to form one-world religion. They decided to pattern this new worldwide church after the Chrislam movement that started in Nigeria in the early

1970s. The Chrislam movement started when pastors in Nigeria decided that Christians and Muslims worshiped the same God. They declared that both the Bible and the Koran were equally anointed and that there was no conflict in the teaching. This movement started out very slowly but gained momentum when some of the megachurch pastors in the United States started embracing the Muslim movement and in the name of peace sought for some common grounds.

It was in the name of peace that the Chrislam movement started, so when the Ambassador of World Peace approached them about working together to establish peace in the world, they quickly submitted to him.

Their Statement of Faith claimed that there was only one God, and while some called him Allah, other called him Jehovah, and still others called him Buddha, all people's Gods were the same.

They named the new religious movement the United Church of World Peace. They elected a hierarchy of officials with the title of World Council of Churches and asked the Ambassador of World Peace to be the chairman of this newly formed council. He quickly accepted this position and brought this new religion under his newly formed department.

With the support of this newly elected church council, his motion to establish a World Police Force appeared to be on the fast track to acceptance.

The only thing that surprised me was our president's opposition to this one World Police Force. Everyone knew he supported a one-world ideology, so it was surprising when he so angrily opposed this motion.

Col. Black told me later that the reason the president so adamantly opposed this motion was that he coveted the position held by the Ambassador of World Peace. Everyone in Washington knew he had always desired to become the world leader. He was very jealous of this man and his supernatural successes, so it was a personal ambition that caused him to object, not the good of America.

Regardless of our president's position and opposition to the motion, the United Nations went ahead and enacted the motion. We now had a World Police Force, and we as a nation were supposed to disband all of our police forces, including the CIA, FBI, Secret Service, and Department of Homeland Security, and bring all local law enforcement agencies under the authority and direction of the World Police Force.

The president continued to oppose this United Nations amendment and refused to submit to this new worldwide agency. Every other nation, with the exceptions of Canada, Mexico, and the United States, submitted to this new World Police Force and embraced the authority of the Ambassador of World Peace. There was tremendous pressure on the president of the United States to conform, but he continued to refuse.

This conflict between the United Nations and the United States reached an untenable level when the United Nations gave the United States an ultimatum. The ultimatum required us to submit to the Ambassador of World Peace and the World Police Force or face worldwide sanctions, including the threat of armed confrontation.

Rumors were rampant claiming that the Ambassador of World Peace was slowly gathering an army of World Police Force soldiers around the United Nations building in New York with the intent of forcing the United States to submit. The Ambassador of World Peace knew if he could force the United States to submit, then Canada and Mexico would quickly follow. The United Nations was supporting the Ambassador of World Peace in his endeavors by hiding the police force inside the United Nations buildings.

Rumors of this pending confrontation quickly spread, and every citizen of the United States was outraged and vowed that we would not surrender to their demands. Average citizens began to grab their weapons and ammo and converged on the United Nations building in New York. Hundreds of thousands of armed citizens had the United Nations surrounded, and we were ready for a fight.

We have had "tent cities" in New York before, but nothing like this one.

In the midst of this confrontation, the president did something so unexpected that he took everyone by surprise. He was so opposed to the amendment establishing the World Police Force that we never gave a thought that he might oppose what we, the citizens, were doing, but he did.

The president declared martial law and ordered the military to disarm the American citizens. The military came in with tanks, armored vehicles, machine guns, and every type of weapon known to man. We the citizens were so outgunned that it was obvious that a massacre was about to take place. The military placed their units between our armed resistance and the United Nations building, and we were looking down the barrel of our military's weapons. American soldiers and American citizens had their weapons aimed at each other. Sons against fathers, friends against friends, all citizens of the United States, and we were about to kill each other.

All of a sudden the commanders of the military gave an order, and the military did an about-face and turned their guns on the United Nations building. The military and the citizens united in confronting the World Peace Force and the Ambassador of World Peace. The World Police Force quickly took refuge inside the United Nations building and sought help from the president of the United States.

The president realized that the military had just mutinied and disobeyed his direct order. He was furious, but he soon came to the realization that he had no other choice but to support the citizens and the military against the United Nations. The standoff was very dangerous, and it appeared as if a major war was ready to breakout. The United Nations was not ready for an armed conflict against a major military force, so they backed down.

As a result of the standoff, the United Nations decided that their tenure on the shores of the United States was over. They gave notice that they were looking for another location in which to set up their headquarters.

ROME

The United Nations, through the Ambassador of World Peace, reached an agreement with the United Church of World Peace to lease facilities that were previously part of the Vatican-owned properties. The United Nations set up their offices just up the road from the Vatican City. Their offices were in a very large commercial building, and the Ambassador of World Peace took over a large facility that had comprised part of the Vatican City.

The Ambassador of World Peace took the top floor of the facilities and also designated two lower floors to house the World Police Force and the United Church of World Peace. The ambassador now had all of those who supported him under one roof, and he began to exercise more stringent control over the actions and decisions of these two organizations.

There were many rumors that the ambassador had more authority than the United Nations and that he was the one who was running the world. I knew this was not true because he still got his power and authority from the United Nations, but he was assuming a lot of power.

In retaliation for the United States' rejection of the amendment forming the World Police Force, the United Nations expelled the United States from the United Nations, and they even went so far as to change their name. The new organization took the name European United Community (EUC), and they reorganized their power structure. The EUC was directed by ten European Nations, and all other nations were just members with no voting rights or real input.

All of these changes took place over nine months, and it was like the world had just given birth to a new ruler.

CHAPTER NINE
DISARMING THE WORLD

The world soon recognized the World Police Force and the power given to the Ambassador of World Peace. The newly formed European United Community enacted new legislation that outlawed the possession of any weapons such as pistols, rifles, or other weapons that expelled a projectile. The list provided by the EUC was very extensive and listed weapons that individuals might possess but also listed weapons that law enforcement or the military might also possess.

The main purpose of this legislation was to disarm the entire world, including individuals but also to disarm governments. The European United Community envisioned a world that was totally disarmed and wherein the only people with weapons were the World Police Force. If they were able to achieve this lofty goal, then the World Police Force could station a small contingency of officers in every nation and maintain peace by force if necessary.

The Ambassador of World Peace would oversee this World Police Force and would be able to enforce any directives issued by the EUC.

The world had just come out of a chaotic period when Russia, Iran, and many other Mideast countries had attacked Israel. South Korea attacked North Korea, and many other armed conflicts had occurred all over the world. No one wanted another war, and the entire world united in this desire for peace. Everyone was saying, "Peace, peace, peace," but everyone was afraid that war would break out again.

The European continent led the way toward worldwide disarmament. Not just the EUC but the entire continent turned in their weapons. The African continent, Asian continent, South America, and almost all other nations followed their example. They began to transport their weapons to Rome, where the Ambassador of World Peace began to stockpile them in warehouses under the protection of the World Police Force. Individuals throughout the entire world began to turn in their weapons to their government, and the governments began turning in their weapons to the World Police Force.

Within six months, the entire world was disarmed, with the exceptions of Canada, Mexico, and the United States.

It was the concept of disarming that caused a wave throughout the North American continent. Understand that our president was in favor of disarming all American citizens. He had even tried when he ordered the military to confiscate all weapons during the standoff at the United Nations building, but the citizens were having no part of this. The president had spent his entire presidency trying to get gun control, but he was unable to achieve this goal.

Americans valued their independence, and throughout the decades and even centuries, American blood had been shed in defense of this independence. We were not going to willingly turn in our weapons to the president who tried to declare martial law. The events at the United Nations proved that we were willing to use them even against the directive of our own president.

Possessing a weapon had always been a sacred right to many American citizens. The second amendment to our Constitution guaranteed every citizen the right to own and bear arms. God, guns, and Mom's apple pie was the basis our great country was founded upon. Many patriotic citizens refused to relinquish those rights, even though God had not been the vogue for many decades.

There was a strong movement by atheists and other ungodly liberals to have the words "in God we trust" removed from our money. They had not succeeded with the money, but they had removed Him from almost every other governmental and public gatherings, publications, and signs. We had fast become a secular society devoid of any belief in God.

Mom's apple pie was replaced by frozen foods, and many moms didn't even cook, so there wasn't even a minor ruckus over that. There was a ruckus when it came to our guns. That was where we drew a line in the sand.

There was a popular bumper sticker that pictured a smoking gun held in someone's hand. The bumper sticker said, "You can have my smoking gun when you can wrestle it out of my dead hand."

We, the citizens of America, became even more defiant regarding possessing guns after the situation at the United Nations. The president's intentions were made clear with that order to disarm the citizens. A new resolve entered into the hearts of Americans that we would not give up our guns and that we would fight to maintain that right.

Over the past decades, there had been many attempts to pass and enforce laws that restricted the types of weapons that civilians could possess. When these attempts failed, they tried to start a national registry so that they would know who had guns and what kind of guns they had. Each time someone tried to pass such a law, the National Rifle Association fought back and was able to get such laws overturned.

The politicians who were trying to disarm America even went so far as to try to enact a law whereby each bullet would have to have a serial number on the casing or the firing pin. The firing pin would transfer this serial number to the casing so that law enforcement could easily find out which gun fired a specific bullet.

The reason politicians gave for this serial-number law was that it would assist law enforcement. If law enforcement recovered a shell casing from the site of a crime, they could then find the gun. The real truth is that they wanted to make it so expensive to produce bullets or firing pins for guns that no one could afford it. They were willing to let us keep our guns if we forced them, but they wanted to stop us from obtaining ammunition.

Our president found out at the United Nations standoff that he could not rule our country until he had disarmed us. He revealed his true intentions when he declared martial law. He wanted to **rule** our country, not **govern** this country, and he was willing to do it by force if necessary.

The European United Community also found out that they could not rule the world until they were able to disarm the three countries in North America, those being Canada, Mexico, and the United States.

Canada had very strict gun laws but was not as attached to their guns as Mexico and the United States. Canada was leaning toward disarming their civilians, but not their military. The Ambassador of World Peace wanted to disarm the military and the police, not just the civilian population.

Mexico, on the other hand, was not about to turn in any weapons, whether military or civilian. Mexico had just come through its civil war, just prior to Russia attacking Israel. The civil war continued even after the Mideast crisis and escalated into a full battle after thousands of people went missing.

The government lost many of their soldiers and government employees in that disaster, but the drug cartels whom they were fighting in the civil war maintained all of their fighters. The government, including the military, was in such disarray after the disappearance of so many people that the drug cartels were able to overcome any resistance quickly and took control of the entire country.

The country was controlled by drug cartels, but it was in such disarray that each cartel controlled a certain area, and they defended their territory by force and by killing anyone who would confront them. The guns gave them power, so there was no way that they were going to disarm. The government did not exist, so there was no one on whom the Ambassador of World Peace could rely to disarm the people.

Americans held on even tighter to our weapons, especially after the fiasco at the United Nations. We knew if the president could get our weapons, he would soon try to take our freedom. Americans started stocking up on ammunition, and many were obtaining the equipment necessary to manufacture our personal ammo. Everyone started hiding their weapons and ammo, but we always kept them nearby and easily accessible.

Even if our president had not tried to declare martial law, there was no way anyone was going to turn in their weapons. We had just come through a period of civil unrest with millions of people suddenly disappearing. The world was in chaos, and now they wanted us to disarm.

That was not going to happen!

The president tried another tactic that I thought was done out of desperation. The Ambassador of World Peace had been trying to get every nation to disarm, and most had done so. The president announced to the United

States that he was also turning in all military weapons and was going to disarm the United States. He said he wanted to set an example and so he, with much fanfare, sent all of our weapons to the Ambassador of World Peace. He then used the argument that the United States was unarmed and no longer was any danger, even to our citizens. He used this action to try to disarm all Americans; he said it behooved all patriotic Americans to submit their personal weapons to the closest military base so that the government could destroy them.

The problem with the president's argument was that Americans were neither stupid nor naïve. We knew that the president had only turned in outdated weapons that were no longer effective. He kept all modern weapons, especially those that were guided by GPS systems, and he hid them in bunkers buried deep in the barren desert.

Private militias started rising up all over the United States with the intent of defending themselves and our precious country if necessary. The government referred to these militias as gangs and even passed new laws making membership in private militias illegal. These militias were necessary to protect ourselves in an ever increasing lawless society in which we now lived.

The World Police Force occasionally made forays into the United States to enforce some archaic law passed by the European United Community, but they were quickly repulsed by the militias.

It reminded me of our American history when we rose up against England and gained independence from tyrannical rule. We had to raise up against these world powers that desired the demise of the United States.

The World Police Force made two forays into Mexico, thinking they would be an easy target, but they soon learned a horrible lesson. The drug cartels slaughtered them and had no mercy on them. When they challenged the drug cartels, the drug cartels extracted a terrible price from the World Police Force.

This movement by the Ambassador of World Peace ended up in a stalemate with Canada, the United States, and Mexico but little did we know that the Ambassador of World Peace would not give up.

CHAPTER TEN
CHIPPED

While we were dealing with the demand by both our government and the European United Community that we, the civilians, disarm, there was more trouble brewing in the background. This new trouble would bring the United States to her knees.

This trouble had been brewing since before World War II, but no one realized the extent of the problem. This problem had to do with the financial practices and the entitlement mentality that started somewhere about 1935 when FDR signed the Social Security Act, originally known as the Economic Security Act. When this program was first implemented it included unemployment compensation, aid to states for welfare and health programs, and aid to dependent children.

This program was followed thirty years later by the Medicare program signed into existence on July 30, 1965. All of these programs filled a need in people's lives, and it was very hard to present an argument against these programs.

It was not the programs that presented the problem; it was the people's response to these programs that brought us to this new crisis. People began to believe that they had a "right" to these benefits rather than it being a privilege to receive them. They lost sight of the fact that this was a government-run program that was designed to help those who were in need. They stopped asking for help or assistance and started demanding these benefits. These recipients even took the government to court demanding the rights that they felt they deserved. There was an entitlement mentality that began to sweep through our society. Psychiatrists even developed a title for this disorder. They called it Narcissistic Personallty Disorder.

I remember one state that required everyone who was receiving unemployment compensation to work on projects that benefited society. The narcissistic recipients of welfare took the state to court, and the judges agreed that it was unreasonable to demand they work in exchange for the benefits. The unemployed men and women went home and got free paychecks for doing nothing. The judge's decision fueled the entitlement mentality that continued sweeping over our nation.

The danger of this entitlement mentality did not reveal itself immediately. It took decades for the evil of this political maneuver to be finally revealed. This movement removed the incentive for hard labor and let everyone know that the government would take care of you and that you were entitled to enjoy the American Dream.

What this society did not take into account was that these programs would expand and would end up costing a lot of money. The government did not make money on its own. They either took it from the citizens by increasing taxes, from a business by increasing fees and regulations, or by borrowing from other nations.

The United States Congress continually raised the taxes on its citizens until it affected the politicians' chances to be reelected. At this time, they stopped taxing citizens and turned to businesses to raise the additional revenue needed to continue these and other entitlement programs. They raised the taxes on businesses so high that many businesses moved overseas. We not only lost the jobs, but we also lost the taxes that these businesses had been paying.

The final source of money was to sell treasury bonds or securities that individuals, business or other nations would purchase. The Treasury Department offered these securities with the promise to pay higher interest at some later date. We spent the money today with the promise of payment later. It didn't take a genius to realize that under this method of entitlement dependency, the National Debt would only increase, and we would owe more and more money to other nations. The only way to lower the National Debt was to lower national spending, and this meant changing our mentality from an entitlement mentality to a self-reliance mentality. To change this mentality meant that we, as citizens, spend only what we earned and what we could afford. To change this mentality also meant that our government stopped borrowing and started balancing the national budget.

Changing our mentality did not mean we stopped helping those in need; it only meant that we stopped making them dependent on the government.

This mentality was what would bring the United States to its knees and would usher in the downfall of the American currency.

AMERICAN ELITISM

America had always been a world leader when it came to the financial arena. They judged the rest of the world by how their currency stacked up to the American dollar, which was the standard, and American enjoyed her elevated status with the highest standard of living in the world. Compared to the rest of the world, Americans had the best of everything.

We had the best cars, the biggest televisions, the largest houses, the best medical care, and the strongest military in the world. No one could defeat our military, but our vulnerability was our financial indiscretion. We had always had a tacit belief in the separation and elitism of the United States. We did not see the United States as part of the world or affected by events that took place on other continents. Oceans, history, and languages separated us, and we did not realize how small the world had become.

We had the mentality that what occurred in Europe only affected Europe and what occurred in Asia affected only Asia. We believed that our institutions, such as banking, depended on our decisions, and what happened in the United States stayed in the United States. The world was changing, but our thinking was not.

This belief was destroyed during the global financial crisis that started in 2006 when the housing bubble in the United States collapsed and the world financial system was heavily damaged. Banks all over the world began to fail, and it was because of the housing market in America.

We asked ourselves how the crash of the American housing market damaged the banks in other nations. The simple fact was that the banks were no longer national banks but had become international. What happened to our banks located in the United States also affected the main branches that were located mainly in the European nations. The bursting of the housing market caused the value of securities tied to the United States real estate pricing to plummet, and this damaged financial institutions globally. Loans were hard to get, and banks suffered a cash loss, which triggered internal safety mechanisms that caused some banks and financial institutions to fall.

The fallout from this crisis caused nations such as Greece, Spain, and Portugal to experience extremely high inflation and caused national crises that many times ended up in civil unrest.

America knew for many years that the homes in America were greatly overpriced and that this bubble was just waiting to burst. We were warned about it, and many economists shouted the alarm, but our government ignored the warnings. In fact, the government was one of the main causes in the massive foreclosures that took place. The cause of this instability was a basic belief that everyone in America was entitled to own a home. Owning a home was referred to as the American Dream.

To facilitate this entitlement, the government guaranteed the housing loans people made on these overpriced residences. The reason the government had to guarantee these loans was that people did not qualify for the homes they wanted and did not want the homes they qualified for.

The government pushed the mortgage companies to accept questionable loans and even made one loan so easy to obtain that the industry referred to the loan as a "liar, liar" loan. The mortgage companies did not even check out the reported income and just accepted the borrowers' written statements as to their income. The government in essence became the cosigners because no self-respecting mortgage lender would have approved such a risky loan without some guarantee.

Everyone knew that the housing bubble would eventually burst, and so it did. Suddenly almost overnight the banking industry was inundated with millions of empty houses, and these foreclosed homes became toxic assets that then cause many banks to collapse. Because the banks were international, the housing burst had ramifications all over the world. The United States suddenly realized that the world's finances were all interwoven, and the American dollar was now just a part of the world finances and no longer the standard on which all other currency rested. We realized that regardless of our desire or belief, there was only the one-world monetary system.

Every nation still had their form of currency, but this also caused worldwide problems because of the balance of trade that was dependent on the value of each nation's currency.

China was a major trading partner for most countries in the world, and because she refused to allow her currency to fluctuate according to the world market, this presented an uneven trading floor.

The United Nations formed the Group of Eight (G8), and the eight most influential and developed countries in the world started meeting and addressing this problem. Their solution was to develop a one-world currency that would replace all existing monetary systems. America was part of the G8 committee and was one of the two nations that opposed this solution. It was our House of Representatives who opposed this idea, while the Senate and the White House supported this one-world currency.

China vetoed this solution because she kept the valuation of her currency at an inflated price because she did not want to lose her trade advantage.

The White House openly supported the one-world currency motion. They even tried to circumvent Congress by writing an executive order but for once both houses of congress stood up against this executive order and were able to stop this unconstitutional grab of power.

It looked like China and the United States standing together would be able to stop this worldwide movement, but something happened that took both China and the United States out of the picture.

NATIONAL DEBT

The United States was able to survive the financial collapse caused by the housing market, and our government kept saying we as a nation were recovering.

The problem with our finances was that our spending was still out of control. Our national debt was still out of control. It was skyrocketing, and every year we were spending trillions more than we were making. The conservatives and the liberals were all warning us that we were on an unsustainable path, and there would soon come a time of accountability when we would reap what we had seeded. They all warned that the results would be disastrous to our nation and to our manner of living.

To finance our entitlement style of living, we were selling more and more Treasury Securities, and the two nations that were buying these securities were China and Japan. America was operating on the assumption that China and Japan were buying these Treasury Securities because they were safe investments. As it turned out, Japan was buying them because they believed in the United States, but China had a different and more sinister motivation.

Our national debt was running over twenty trillion dollars and growing by trillions each year. There was a lot of talk about China owning the United States and what would happen if China decided to rid herself of the securities. Along with the securities, she would dump all of the American dollars she had stored in her banks on the international market all at one time. The standard conclusion was that it would cause the American dollar to lose value and would cause uncontrolled inflation that would destroy America and make the dollar worth nothing.

A quick check showed that China only owned 8 percent of the national debt, or roughly 1.6 trillion. The part that we overlooked was that the Social Security Administration owned 16 percent of the national debt, and the Federal Reserve Bank owned an additional 12 percent, with Japan owning 7 percent. Creative bookkeeping made our national debt appear to be approximately twenty trillion, but in reality it was at least 30 percent higher.

I only give these facts to show how deep the hole was we had dug. Even though China only owned 8 percent, the result of her dumping those securities on the open market would have a greater effect because of the creative bookkeeping that we were using. Even though we looked at all the possibilities, no one thought that China would follow through on her threat. We believed this because it would also destroy their financial system and cause just as great inflation in China as it did in the United States.

If China followed through on her threat, she would cause a huge financial disaster in the United States, but China would also fall. No one believed that China or Japan would flood the world market with the securities, but we assumed that China was a rational nation, and as events proved later, she was not.

Unbeknownst to us, China thought that she could use the Treasury Securities as a weapon to control the United States. She thought that if she could stockpile enough American dollars and Treasury Bonds, the United States would have to submit to her out of fear. This fear would provide China with a formidable weapon with which to threaten the United States. After all, what rational nation would do something that would destroy its economy and cause extreme inflation?

China and the United States involved themselves in a war of brinksmanship, with each trying to outdo the other. It was like a game of Russian roulette between these two nations, but much more was at stake, and the outcome would affect the entire world.

To better understand China, we must understand her history. China believed that the dragon had come to her and prophesied that she would rule the world. She would not conquer the world with war and weapons but through business and finances.

This belief created a society whereby the highest calling a man could have was to own his successful business empire and expand that business into other nations. As I explained before when I was talking about the Cold War, we saw evidence of China in the Mideast, Africa, and in all other nations that would accept help. China's expansion was during the Cold War, and it had only increased over the decades since the Cold War ended.

China also made great inroads into the United States by buying businesses and taking over the import/export trade. They also began to buy up properties, including homes and businesses. The United States was one of the few countries where you did not have to be a citizen to buy and own property.

Under United States laws, a businessman had to invest $500,000 dollars and hire a certain number of employees to obtain a green card. He had to guarantee this continued investment for a certain number of years, and then he would be guaranteed green papers that would allow him to work. He could then buy property, and it is a proven fact that the Chinese were able to take over entire cities in various locations in California and even in other states.

Another method they used was to find a failing contractor who was ready to go bankrupt. They would offer to buy a controlling interest in the company and leave the original owner as president. The original owner had the contractor's license, but the new immigrants had a controlling interest. This company was now able to bid on governmental contracts that were awarded to minority-owned businesses, so they slowly took over a large amount of the contracting business.

Over the last few decades, the Chinese dominated the import/export businesses, manufacturing businesses, large contracting businesses, and even property renovation. The Chinese plan was taking place, and through businesses they were taking over the United States, one property at a time.

Most of the profits went back to China, and they used our money to buy the United States Treasury Bonds and also to stockpile American dollars in their banks. The balance of trade between the United States and China was extremely lopsided in favor of the Chinese, so they made even more money in the trading markets.

The real motive for China buying the Treasury Bonds was to dominate and control the United States. They believed by buying enough of the United States bonds they could control decisions the United States made and could eventually control the United States and Canada, where they used the same strategy.

China's final goal was to control the European United Community by forcing the United States and Canada to join with them. Together she would have such power that the European United Community would be forced to submit to the Chinese demands. If China could accomplish her goal, she would, in essence, rule the world, and the dragons prophesy would be achieved.

When China felt the time was ripe, she issued a letter of demand ordering the United States and Canada to support China's position with the European United Community. By us supporting China's position, it would give control to China, and she would then dictate what took place in the entire world. The plot may sound preposterous, but it had every chance of working if the United States and Canada put their entire support behind China.

The letter of demand included a veiled threat about selling all of the United States Bonds and dumping all of the American dollars on the banking scene. The United States had never responded well to threats, so our government's immediate response was to forget it.

China responded with a more lethal demand accompanied by a total of the United States Treasuries Bonds that it held and also the total amount of United States currency that was in Chinese banks. They simply asked, "What would happen if we suddenly found it necessary to dispose of our United States holding?"

Our president, who was viewed as a paper tiger because he was quick on threats and slow on action, immediately issued another executive order placing an embargo on all trade with China. China did not react publically, but I know there were all sorts of diplomacy taking place behind the scenes.

China refused to back down, and after waiting for two months, she followed through on her threats. She flooded the money market with American dollars and sold or demanded payment on all of the bonds that she possessed. China did the unbelievable action, and the effect on the American monetary system was instant and disastrous.

The credit rating for the United States Treasury Bonds went from "good" to "extremely poor." No country would buy our Treasury Bonds, and each country began to dump their stockpile of American dollars. They inundated the market with American dollars, and this action did cause immediate inflation. United States currency became almost worthless, and the United States went from one of the richest nations with the highest per-capita living standards to one of the poorest nations in the world.

The United States was unable to pay even the interest on her debts, and the United States went into default.

China suffered almost the same fate, as she also endured uncontrollable inflation, and her currency also became almost worthless.

The European United Community took immediate advantage of this situation and called for an emergency meeting of the Group of Twenty with the intent of forcing a one-world monetary system in the world. Ordinarily the meeting would have been the Group of Eight, but with China and the United States out of the picture, the European United Community felt they needed the representation of the largest group they could convene. They purposed placing this one-world system under the direct control of the Ambassador of World Peace to be implemented and enforced by the World Police Force and the World Justice Courts.

China and the United States were both excluded from the meeting partly because of the financial situation. It was also because both nations refused to submit to the leadership of the European United Community or the Ambassador of World Peace. The Group of Twenty used China and the United States as an example of why the world needed one worldwide currency and what would happen when nations would not submit to the Ambassador of World Peace.

The European United Community passed a motion instructing the active members of the Group of Eight to develop a worldwide monetary system and demanded that it be operational in three and a half years.

ONE WORLD MONETARY SYSTEM

The G8 committee started meeting in Rome with the express purpose of developing a new system and committed to having it operational in less than the allotted three and a half years. The monetary system would be revolutionary in design and would easily be controlled by the European United Community.

The United Nations was dissolved when they were forced out of the United States and were replaced by a group of ten European nations referred to as the European United Community. This group, along with the Ambassador of World Peace, took the lead in developing this one-world currency. The reason Europe took the lead in developing the new world currency was because the world powers were all located in Europe. The United States and China, and to some extent Japan, were no longer relevant.

I remembered when the housing market burst, a team of economists from Harvard predicted the necessity of a new world monetary system based on a standard other than the existing gold standard. They did not even try to guess what this new system would be based on but stated that we needed to start fresh and to think out of the box. It now seemed that the team from Harvard was very prophetic in their predictions.

The European United Community took the lead in developing this new system, but it was obvious to me that the Ambassador of World Peace was the main force behind the decisions. The ambassador's involvement became even more obvious when the European United Community announced that the enforcement of these new rules would fall under the authority of the World Police Force as overseen by the Ambassador of World Peace.

It was obvious to me that the Ambassador of World Peace was quickly becoming a world dictator. He now controlled most of the communications and almost all of the international weapons. He also controlled the World Police Force, the United Church of World Peace, and the World Justice Courts, and now he was trying to dominate the world's financial system.

I didn't understand why the world did not recognize what was happening. Why were they all going along with this man, who clearly planned on ruling the world? China and Japan tried to fight the move to a one-world currency. However, both countries, along with the United States, were forced to submit to the dictates of the Ambassador of World Peace in agreement with the European United Community. It is ironic that what brought down both countries was the American debt.

China brought down America, and in return America's debt brought down China, but Japan was the innocent victim of this power struggle between China and the United States. Innocent or not, Japan still fell.

With Russia physically destroyed and the United States, China, and Japan financially ruined, there was no one to block the monetary coup. The coup was staged by the European United Community under the direction of the Ambassador of World Peace.

The European United Community decreed that the system was to be fully operational in three and a half years but would start implementing it within a few months. I believed the timetable for the world monetary system was that the first draft would be completed within six months. The revised draft would be completed within one year, and the implementation would begin six months after the completion of the final draft.

To maintain peace and help settle the fears of the people, negotiations over the one-world currency took place in complete secrecy. It took place under the watchful eyes of the World Police Force and the Ambassador of World Peace.

Few details leaked out, but I knew that there were conversations about how to control this monetary system. They discarded anything to do with the modern system, such as credit or debit cards, because they could be forged or stolen. They also discarded any technology that was connected to the Internet or cell phones, as it was totally unreliable and went offline too often.

They wanted to implement a system that could not be stolen or misused and would always be with the person. They wanted it to be immediately accessible and without any authorization from the user. They wanted a system that could track the user and automatically updated their account regardless of where they were or what they were doing.

One of the technologies they were investigating was the eye recognition system that was already in development and had proven to be reliable. Everyone's eyes were like fingerprints; they were unique to that individual, and we had the technology to implement this system within six to seven months.

They were also looking at the face recognition system that could scan thousands of people in a crowd and identify each one instantly. This system was also foolproof and could also be used to keep track of everyone's location through a complex system of cameras. All the technology was also readily available, and with some upgrades would have all the capabilities that they required.

The final system they were looking at was the implanted digital chip that could be scanned by simple machines and maintain millions of files that could be downloaded whenever that person passed a scanning machine.

The good part about this chip system was that part of the Affordable Care Act required everyone to have a chip implanted in their wrist or on their forehead. This chip contained all of these people's medical records as well as their insurance plans and was instantly attainable by the doctors and hospitals.

These chips were proven to save people's lives and had prevented mix-ups in the emergency rooms that had also saved many people's lives.

There was an added benefit to these implanted chips about which the officials were not talking. In the past few years, many people had been kidnaped by terrorist groups and held for ransom in unknown locations. In the earlier decades before the chips, it was difficult to locate the kidnaped people, and many people died because ransoms were not paid. The chip could locate a person within a two-square-foot area. If the kidnaped person was chipped, officials could locate them instantly, and the law enforcement team could rescue them.

The reason they were not talking about this capability was that the officials could, with the right software, keep track of everyone's movements, and there would be no privacy and no secrets.

What people didn't realize was that this was presently taking place. Everyone who had a cell phone, and almost everyone did, was constantly tracked. Every time a cell-phone user moved locations into another cell-phone tower range, the new tower recorded their location along with the time and any calls they might make from this new location.

It was a known fact that specifically in the Los Angeles area, private investigators located false towers that appeared to be for cell-phone usage. They easily passed the scrutiny of the common traveler, who assumed that they were just common towers. These towers were not for cell phones, and no one would acknowledge who put them up and what purpose they were fulfilling. We could only extrapolate that some unknown governmental agency put them in place, and they were used for gathering private information. If a federal agency did not put them in place, then the local cities would require a permit to install these towers. The local city would then have copies of the permits, including who installed them and what the purpose was.

The fact that investigators could not locate a permit or even identify the agency behind the towers indicates that they belonged to a secret governmental agency.

We didn't know what the outcome of this one-world monetary system would be, but it would have a sinister purpose.

CHAPTER ELEVEN
EARTHQUAKES

It had been approximately a year and a half since Russia invaded Israel, and still disaster after disaster was striking the earth. It happened all over the world, and not one nation or continent had been spared, with the exception of Israel. Israel suffered some damage, but compared to the rest of the world, she had been extremely lucky. It was almost as if Russia's invasion of Israel opened Pandora's box, and now every demon (if you believed in them) was running loose and wreaking havoc.

This world as my wife and my family knew it no longer exists. When my wife was alive, the United States was the superpower controlling much of what occurred throughout the world. Under the direction of our president, we withdrew our troops from all other nations, and our only military presence was within our own borders.

One of our closest allies, Mexico, experienced a civil war between the drug cartels and the Mexican Army. The drug cartels, fighting with weapons provided to them by our government, ATF, FBI, and CIA, quickly defeated the Mexican Army and soon controlled all of Mexico.

The president, under the pretext of protecting our borders from these drug cartels, stationed our military along the border between Mexico and the United States, and quickly the porous border was finally sealed.

The president would not give up on his desire to disarm all of us and with the support of the ruling political party enacted a new law whereby every citizen was required to turn in all weapons. Weapons were defined as "any device that propels a projectile that has the potential to injure, maim, frighten, or kill any human being or other protected species." The weapons were to be deposited at any governmentally approved center, and failure to obey this executive order would be dealt with in the harshest manner.

The president's new law was a continuation of the European United Community's efforts to disarm every citizen and every government. Now our president was taking the lead in the United States because he realized he couldn't become a dictator so long as the average citizen was armed.

The majority of pacifistic, pathetic citizens were eagerly obeying these orders without looking at the consequences, and they were blinded by a mistaken belief in the innate goodness of our governmental leadership. We never seemed to learn a lesson.

I was contacted by Col. Black, and he advised our entire Special Ops team to hide our weapons, but keep them within reach. His operatives informed him that our president's sole purpose in confiscating the weapons was to remove any threat to his consolidation of power. He was intent on using the world crisis to proclaim himself to be a dictator and to rule the United States without opposition. He was heard to say laughingly, "Don't let a good crisis go to waste."

I immediately hid my weapons and stored my ammunition in a very safe and secure location. It quickly became obvious from the increase in violence, specifically home and business invasions, that only the lawful citizens had surrendered their weapons, and the criminals were still very well armed. Gangs were starting to claim their territories and were now openly carrying weapons and intimidating the citizens.

Our local law enforcement agencies were too busy to patrol the streets, so gangs and criminals started to enforce their own laws. There was no one in authority who would even question me on carrying a weapon, so I felt very safe packing heat. I did hide my larger weapons and ammo, but I could easily conceal my automatic, so I kept that with me.

The city I lived in had been spared from any violence so far, but I still packed heat (Smith and Wesson, M&P) whenever I left my house.

I was trying to live as normal a life as I could, but there had been many days that I was just overwhelmed by loneliness and regrets. I had a deep desire to just get away from everything human and to enjoy some solitude in the mountains that surround my little community.

One special Wednesday seemed like one of those days, so I decided early in the morning to take my backpack and some food and water and hike into the San Gabriel Mountains, which were almost in my backyard. It took me a couple of hours to hike to the ridge just south of Mt. Wilson, but I found the ideal spot to soak in the sun and refresh myself emotionally.

I found a rock on an overlying ridge that oversaw the entire Los Angeles basin. The morning's sun was just warming up the rocks, and with the early morning stillness it was the perfect place just to sit and reflect.

My thoughts immediately went to my wife, my family and the wonderful years that we had together after I retired from Special Ops.

Oh, how I missed them!

I missed the special times when Sandy, Lulu, and I would sit on the porch in the evenings, just reflecting on good things. Sometimes I would just sit and look at her and marvel at what a wonderful wife she was. I could never have asked for a more loving and caring wife and one who would stand beside me even if she didn't understand what I was doing.

Lulu would be curled up on the floor at our feet, and she would usually place herself in a position where she could watch us as we sat on the porch in those special rocking chairs. She would not move her head. She would only move her eyes between Sandy and me. If we said anything to her, she would get up and sit right at our feet, waiting for us to scratch her neck or rub her back.

I felt so alive during these special times. The love that surrounded me was so great and was something I needed more than anything else in the world.

Even as I sat there on that rock, sadness and loneliness enveloped me as I knew I would never feel anything like that again. I would never have anyone I loved again, and deep down I knew that I didn't deserve anyone. I knew I had better come to grips with my solitary life.

I did have a lot of regrets. I wished I had been a better husband, father, and grandfather. I wished I had spent the time I had with family, rather than on things that in the long run didn't really matter and did not really change anything in the course of history.

I remembered one verse from the Bible that I was forced to memorize when I attended Sunday school. That verse was somewhere in Ecclesiastes and went something like this: "Vanity of vanities, all is vanity," and right in the same general location it talked about "grasping for the wind."

I felt like those two passages described my life and my priorities. I was grasping for something that seemed real to me at the time but in the long scheme of things really didn't mean anything.

I was always involved in secret missions that at the time seemed so important and vital to national security, but now seems so frivolous. I didn't regret what I did in the past; I just realized that I missed out on so much with my family and friends.

As I was lying on that rock reflecting on the past, I realized that I missed out on what was the most important thing in my life, and that was family. As I realized how important and wonderful those things were, I also realized that I would never again enjoy either family or the love that they shared with me.

I must and I would deal with these facts, and I would continue to make myself available to Col. Black in the hope that I could somehow alter the future. I wanted to help alter the future so that the next generation could salvage something for their children. It was too late for me, but maybe the next generation would learn from these mistakes.

I knew that the America that I grew up in was gone and would never return. I also knew that the world had entered the path of no return, and this left Canada and the United States to determine the future of the North American Continent. At some point, we would have to confront the European, Asian and African continents and any other nations that supported the Ambassador of World Peace. The outcome of that confrontation would determine the future of the world.

As I contemplated the future of the world, I experienced the same emotions that I used to experience just prior to embarking on a Special Ops mission. I was trying to put all emotions aside and force myself to relax and quietly wait for the orders to embark on a mission. The problem was I didn't know what the mission would be, and I had no idea when this mission would take place, but I knew it would happen.

I used to take a hike and enjoy some solitude and peacefulness in preparation for a mission. That is what I was doing while I was lying on that rock and enjoying the warm sun and the many small animals that were playing on the forest grounds that surrounded that rock.

I decided that I could not alter the past, and I could not remove the regrets so I would only concentrate on the future and whatever part I would have in it.

It was with these thoughts in my mind that I started to relax and appreciate the environment in which I lived. It was a warm day with only a slight breeze blowing through the trees. I was lying on a very large rock listening to the chirping of the birds and the quiet rustling of the little chipmunks as they scurried among the fallen leaves. It was so relaxing that I could feel myself slowly sinking into a restful sleep when suddenly an eerie silence permeated the peaceful forest.

I had trained myself to listen to the sounds that surrounded me because they were the first signs of pending danger. When I used to spend time in the jungle, I would stop and just listen. The jungle was alive with sounds and so long as I heard the natural sounds of the jungle, I knew it was safe.

I was so attuned to the natural sounds of the jungle that any deviation from those sounds would automatically warn me of danger. Even though I was almost asleep, the silence immediately woke me, and I was ready to confront any danger.

The chirping of the birds had stopped, and all of the scurrying chipmunks had stopped in the tracks. Everything was looking south toward the Los Angeles basin. I glanced at the sky, expecting to see a soaring hawk, but my gaze was quickly drawn back to the valley floor. Dread filled my heart as I witnessed a sight I had only seen once before.

I saw circular rings of dust spreading out across the canyon floor headed in my direction. The best way I could describe these rings was to use the example of when I would stand on the banks of a quiet mountain lake and throw a rock out into the still water.

A circular ring would emit from the point of impact that would then spread out until the force of the impact was dissipated. This same phenomenon was taking place but now it was on dry land, not a pond.

I knew these rings were the results of a very large earthquake, and I could see them headed in my direction. I could see that the epicenter was somewhere near the high-rise buildings at Third and Spring Streets in the middle of downtown Los Angeles. I knew the force of this earthquake would reach me very soon.

It was a strange feeling to know that shortly the force of this gigantic earthquake would be upon me, and there was nothing I could do to escape its fury.

Even as I contemplated this earthquake, the rock I stood on suddenly moved out from under me, and I fell approximately five feet to the ground. The fall knocked the wind out of me, and I hit my left side on a large limb that was lying on the ground. I gasped for air and tried to regain my footing, but every time I rolled over, I was knocked to the ground again.

The whole earth around me was shaking, and it felt like I was in the middle of a tsunami. The slope that I was standing on was now rushing toward the valley floor, just like it was water. It was totally dry, but the rocks and debris created a large landslide, and I was caught in the middle of the slide. There were rocks crashing all around me, and I was getting battered by all types of debris, including the large rocks, but I didn't feel any pain.

After what seemed like an eternity, the shaking stopped, and I came to a standstill, reasonably still intact. I lay on the ground for an extended period as I tried to regain my breath and also take stock of my arms and legs to see if I broke anything. I received numerous cuts and abrasions, but I didn't seem to have broken anything.

There was an eerie quietness about me, and the only sounds I heard were rocks settling into position. I remember in college the professor asking the question about a tree falling in the forest with no one around and if it would have made any noise. The professor's question came back to me because when everything was falling and crashing, I didn't remember any sounds. I remembered my thoughts and seeing the landslide, but for the life of me I could not remember any sounds.

As I surveyed the extensive damage around me, I knew that this was no ordinary earthquake. I had experienced earthquakes in the magnitude of 7.2, but I instinctively knew that this was far larger than that.

I could not determine my exact location because the earthquake had stirred up so much dust I could barely see twenty or thirty feet away. I could not see the valley floor, but I was starting to hear some faint noises that could be distant screams, but I could not make them out. I could hear what could be explosions or collapsing structures, and I could make out what seemed to be alarm systems going off, but I could not be sure. It was strange hearing faint noises but not being able to see anything.

The dust was beginning to settle, and I knew I was not going to travel anywhere until I had my bearings and some sense of what I faced. I was just going to remain on that mountainside until the dust had settled enough for me to evaluate the situation, and then I would decide on my course of action.

I didn't know how long it had been, but the dust had settled enough for me to see the worst sight I had ever seen. I could see the valley floor where the high-rise buildings used to be, but all I could see was a pile of debris with smoke and flames shooting from it. Not one high-rise was standing, and I could not even make out one building that seemed to be intact. I could not see the details, but I could make out flames and plenty of smoke. The flames were shooting at least one hundred feet into the air, and it looked like the oil wells in Kuwait after we drove the Iraqis from the land.

There must have been hundreds if not thousands of separate fires scattered all over the valley floor, and the smoke was forming a blanket over the entire basin.

As I scanned the entire valley, I could see off to my left a wall of water and debris burst out of the area I knew was Azusa Canyon. I knew instinctively that the reservoirs in the canyon were destroyed, and millions of gallons of water had suddenly been released. I knew that the canyon was inhabited with new subdivisions, and from prior experiences, I knew the houses had all been destroyed by the wall of water. These homes and their residents were now part of that wall of debris. I could only imagine how many men, women, and children had been killed by that disaster alone.

I believed that I could see enough to have some sense of what I would be facing when I got to my residence or what remained of my residence. I decided to leave the mountain and slowly make my way down that hill.

As I was slowly making my way down that mountainside, it was strange, but many of the rocks that were dislodged by the earthquake were still rolling down the mountain side. It seemed like I continually played dodgeball with boulders that were intent on killing me. I had many close calls, but I managed to dodge them all.

I was so relieved to see the base of the foothills and to reach the first level of what used to be homes, but I was dismayed by the extreme destruction that I was witnessing. I expected to see the extensive damage, but not 100 percent destruction. There was not one house remaining intact, and many of them were on fire.

People were frantically digging through the debris, trying to find their loved ones, but the flames were devouring the wooden structures almost before the neighbors searched them. I felt sorry for the survivors, but I could not make a real difference in any of their lives, so I just continued to my neighborhood.

I did stop and help one elderly lady who was hysterically pulling at some beams that were lying on top of her husband. Together we were able to free him, and I helped move him to a location near the street in case medical aid was to arrive, but to me he did not seem to be seriously injured.

It was obvious to me that hundreds of people had been killed just in my neighborhood alone and many thousands more in the rest of the city. I cannot adequately describe the chaos around me. Desperate people were screaming for help, crying in pain, and hugging their dead and injured, while all around us homes were burning. Water was shooting into the air from broken water mains, gas pipes were leaking, and small explosions were taking place as the released gas ignited.

People were taking their injured family members and placing them near the street in hopes that emergency personnel would arrive. They never realized that we were isolated and no one could make it in or out. The earthquake had stranded us, and our survival would now depend on who was prepared and who wasn't.

We had been warned about the "great earthquake" that one day would strike the Los Angeles area simply because we lived on active earthquake faults. The experts advised us to be prepared to survive for at least three days because that was how long it would take for help to arrive. Most of the people had ignored these warnings, and very few had prepared for any disaster, let alone an earthquake of this magnitude. I did not know how long it would be before help arrived, but I suspected it would be weeks before we saw anyone outside of our immediate neighbors.

When I arrived at my residence, all I saw was a pile of debris. I immediately went to a metal container that I used for storage. It was a large twenty-by-twelve-by-twelve container, and I had stockpiled survival equipment in that container for years. I knew that eventually a large earthquake would occur, so I made sure I prepared for the worst.

I had tents, food, water, first-aid supplies, and, most importantly, I kept my Smith and Wesson 9mm automatic and my AR15, along with a large supply of ammo, safely stashed in that container. I knew that if safety personnel were unable to reach us, it wouldn't be long before marauding gangs of criminals would form and begin to prey upon the helpless survivors. I was not going to be one of those helpless survivors.

I set up my tent in a vacant church parking lot next to my destroyed residence. The parking lot was very close to the metal container, so it was easy to do. The metal container protected my back, and the parking lot protected my front. No one could get to me without my seeing them, and with an automatic pistol and a rifle, I knew I was safe.

I placed a few sandbags in front of my tent so that I could hide behind them, and my fortress was now complete.

I strapped on my pistol, and I started carrying my AR15 so that everyone could see that I was armed and ready to repel any unwanted people. A few of the neighbors cautiously approached me and asked if they could stay near me. I could see they were afraid. I told them to go and gather a few mattresses and blankets from the destroyed residences, along with chairs, and I let them form a little camp near where I placed my tent.

I did not want them around me, but I knew that I would need their help (eyes and ears) if assistance did not come soon. We waited for over one week, and we never even saw a sign that help was on the way.

We never saw a helicopter, a fixed-wing aircraft, or any other type of vehicle. There were neither police officers nor firemen, and even though I thought the National Guard would eventually come, it never happened.

After a week, it became obvious that we were on our own and that help was not coming. During the week we were waiting, I scavenged among the wrecked homes and was able to obtain canned food and other necessary supplies before the trips became too dangerous.

The first thing I did after a few of the neighbors joined me was to form a small team of men and women to make a foraging trip to the supermarket that was located two blocks from my camp. The supermarket was destroyed, but I knew we could get some needed supplies. I wanted to get there before others started looting the store so that the small group with me could survive. We had obtained a lot of nonperishable food, extra water, and even toilet paper before others began to take advantage of this destroyed market.

As we were getting ready to leave the store with our supplies, I almost laughed when one of my neighbors asked if we would get into trouble for stealing from the market. I told them if it concerned them, they could leave a note at the cash register telling them what we had taken and that we would return with payment. I even offered to leave a check for the approximate amount. The sad part was while I was facetious, these people were serious.

We made a number of trips to the store, but the last trip I took to the market proved to me that we had made our last trip because the situation was too dangerous. I saw two people get into an argument over a can of food, and the argument ended with one man stabbing the other man and then running away as a group of people chased him while throwing rocks at him.

People were in desperate need of food and water, and we were still within the first week. I knew from experience that the situation would escalate if help did not arrive soon. The strong would begin to prey on the weak, and the "normal" people would begin to form gangs. Territories would be staked out, and some of the people would begin to arm themselves. This phenomenon was already taking place even before the earthquake.

Once gangs began to arm themselves, it was only a matter of time before people begin to die. Without laws, the lawless become ruthless, and anarchy begins to rule.

These gangs started out as neighbors gathering together for protection and support, but as food and water became scarce and life hung in the balance, survival became the only law, and force became the only tool.

I tried to explain this process to those who gathered around me, but they kept saying that we were a civilized nation and that people would not sink that low. I told them the only reason they were not involved in this fighting was that I had provided them with food and water. They were neither starving nor in need of water. All of their basic needs were being met. They still could not come to grips with the reality of society.

They changed their minds about our city being civilized approximately two weeks after I had this conversation with them. One night shortly after the sun had set, we heard gunfire in the proximity and then the screaming from at least two people. I knew it was two people because one was a woman's voice, and one was a man's voice. The man was begging for their lives and for the gang to leave them alone. This begging was futile, and all we heard was laughter and two final shots.

The next morning I took two men with me, and we tried to find the victims of the previous night's violence. Two blocks to our east we found the couple huddled together, lying on the front porch of their house. They were both dead. The stark reality of violence hit our little group hard, but they needed to realize that we were living in a lawless society right now, where the strong (better armed) ruled.

After we had become aware of the murders, I organized our little group into teams, and we formed a perimeter around our little camp. The men were all placed in strategic locations so that they could call me if any of the gangs tried to infiltrate us. A few times some of the gangs tried to come closer than I wanted them to, so I placed a few AR15 rounds near their feet, and they quickly retreated.

We maintained our location for about one month, and then we begin to run short of water and food. The gangs were also starting to get bolder, and almost on a nightly basis I had to repel at least one gang.

One night a rival gang decided they would kill me, so in the darkness of night one gang member tried to assassinate me. He crawled close to our perimeter line and then suddenly opened fire on me with a rifle.

One of our perimeter guards had spotted him crawling close, so I was ready to react to any aggression that he might perpetrate. When he opened fire, I immediately laid down suppressing gunfire that forced him to hide behind a pile of debris. While he had his head down, I moved into a position where I had a clear lane of fire. As he raised his rifle again, I quickly sighted in on his leg, specifically his knee, and carefully placed one .223-caliber round through his knee cap.

He dropped his rifle and began to scream as he grabbed his left leg. I knew his leg was shattered by my AR15 round, but I wanted him wounded, not dead. Each time one of his fellow gang members tried to reach him I would put another round as close to their heads as I could. I wanted them to be afraid of me, and I wanted them to know that I would kill anyone who made an attack on this small encampment.

I finally let them pull him to safety, and we knew from the screams of pain that he would not be harassing anyone very soon. It was my professional option that he would die soon, not from the wound but from the infection that would soon develop.

The gang's ambush was the most blatant attack against us, but I knew there would be much more if we remained in our present encampment. We were too exposed, and there was very little cover and concealment, so I felt it was necessary to move.

I gathered our little community together and told them what I was planning and why I felt we needed to move now. Some of the members questioned the wisdom of moving out of our location and perhaps miss out on the rescue teams, but I reminded them that we had no idea when or if they would arrive. I also had them gather up the food and water we had remaining, and it became very obvious to everyone that we would run out of food and water within a couple of days.

I told them that we had no choice but to leave, and still about half of the group decided to remain. They asked me where we were going, and I only told them into the mountains beyond the foothills. I refused to reveal the exact location, but I told them that we could see the city and would be able to see if rescuers arrived.

I told them that when rescuers arrived, we would return when we knew it was safe, but until then we were going to remain in the mountains. I asked those who were remaining what they were planning on eating and drinking, and they said, "Surely someone will share with us."

I reminded them of the murders we had already witnessed and the latest attack on our lives, but they refused to accept the fact that humans could be such animals devoid of compassion. I found out later that many of them were mad at me because I put a bullet into the leg of my attacker, and they felt that I was responsible for the violence that was surrounding us.

Some of the men held a private meeting while I was out patrolling the neighborhood, and they convinced some of our community that diplomacy was the best course of action. They believed that we needed to put our guns down and peacefully dialogue with the armed gangs.

I was so fed up with these pacifists that I told them I would leave half the food and water with them. If anyone wanted to go with me, they could pack up their tents, sleeping bags, and whatever else they wanted to take, We would be leaving in half an hour.

After the allotted time, I headed into the mountains and noticed that only five other people followed me, and approximately fifteen stayed behind.

Some of them once again asked me where we were going, but again I did not want to reveal our new location, which would have jeopardized our safety. I just told them we were going to the mountains to escape the violence around us.

Years ago when I was hiking in the mountains, I started exploring a short, dead-end canyon when I found a well-hidden abandoned gold mine tucked away behind some dense chaparral and green bushes. The canyon was L-shaped, but you could not see the L because of the chaparral and brush.

I could tell that no one had been in the mine for decades because the brush was thick, and there was no trail leading to it. It was totally by accident that I found the mine because when I was ten feet from the opening, I still could not see it. The only reason I found the opening was I saw a rabbit just ahead of me, and suddenly it disappeared around what was obviously a corner. I went around the corner, and suddenly there was an opening to a mine.

The opening was well supported by thick bracing made of six-by-six timbers, and the entire interior of the mine shaft was solidly braced. I felt it was totally safe, so I took the time to explore the entire mine.

There were three levels of the mine that were each accessed by descending on wooden ladders. The bottom level had a clear pool of cold water that was fed by an underground stream, and with the right supplies, a person or persons could survive for a long time and never have to leave the mine.

The mine was approximately a quarter of a mile deep, and it had two right-angle bends that would make the mine easy to defend if one of the gangs tried to enter the mine shaft and attack us.

It was to this mine that I decided to seek shelter along with my team. I was worried about the safety of the mine shaft after the great earthquake we had just experienced. When we reached the mine opening, I could see that the bracing was still intact, and the mine was quite safe.

It was interesting to see the expressions on the faces of my team when we made a left turn that exposed the entrance to the mine, and suddenly they became aware of where I had been taking them.

We entered the mine shaft, and I had them drop their survival equipment on the floor and invited them to explore the mine with me. I did this so that I could see who was afraid of dark places and who I could count on to run the operation if I had to leave for any length of time.

Only two of the team could bring themselves to climb the ladders and reach the third level where the water was, but I did have two members on whom I could count. They were extremely surprised to see the cold water, and when they found that it was drinkable, they were highly encouraged.

We remained hidden in the mine shaft for two days while we set up our camp in the mine. My team expressed concern because our food supply was running out, and they suggested that we make a trip into the city and scavenge for food. I told them it was too dangerous but that I would get some meat for all of us.

I hiked further into the canyon until I was at least two miles from our camp, and then I started hunting for some of the deer that inhabited these mountains. I knew that the earthquake would not have frightened them away because they liked to feed on the rose bushes in the front yards of the homes in our city. I had often seen them in the early morning hours brazenly walking down the streets, and I knew which canyons they used in their trek to the bushes.

I quietly entered the canyon and hid behind some trees until I saw a small deer that was approximately fifty feet away from me. I quickly shot her, butchered her, loaded the meat onto my shoulders, and hiked back to the mine. I was careful to make sure that no one was trailing me, and I was very careful to make sure I was not leaving any footprints.

We started a small fire with very dried wood so as to not make any smoke, and we cooked all of the deer meat we had. The deer meat lasted us almost three days, as we kept it in the coldest part of the mine, and with the water we had, we ate very well.

Every three days I had to go out on another hunting trip, but everything was working out very well. I was very surprised that I never ran across anyone while I was hunting, but everyone seemed to be staying in the city.

We were able to maintain this lifestyle for a couple of months until I finally spotted a military helicopter flying low over the city. I left the safety of the mine and made my way back to the city. I found that the military had finally established control, and I felt that the team could safely return to their homes. We then broke up, and made our own ways into what was left of our city and our homes.

I remained in the mine shaft for another couple of weeks, contemplating what had happened, and then I decided it was necessary for me to return to the abandoned church parking lot where our adventure had started.

CHAPTER TWELVE
WORLD POWER STRUGGLE

I was so involved in my struggle just to survive the great earthquake that I was oblivious to the power struggle that was taking place in the world.

As things began to stabilize in our local community, I began to take notice of the world situation once again. My attention returned to the world situation mainly because of a call from Col. Black, who instructed us to watch China and to be aware of the jockeying for power that was taking place. Col. Black felt that this power struggle was a danger to America and would eventually overtake us and force us to make a decision concerning our allegiance.

There were three main nations or coalitions struggling to exert themselves as the dominant world power. The three were the European United Community, China, and the United States/Canada.

Russia was eliminated as a result of the attack on Israel, and so only three remained. The active fight seemed to be between the European United Community and China. The United States chose to remain silent and to observe the fight but not to get involved in the dispute.

PHYSICAL HARDSHIPS AFTER THE GREAT QUAKE

Let me explain what the local situation was before and during this world power struggle. It truly seemed to me that this world was coming to an end. People had always predicted doom and gloom, but their worst predictions didn't even hold a candle to what was happening.

I will try to describe for you what we experienced on a daily basis. There was an unbearable stench that surrounded us and was so strong that you could almost cut it with a knife.

There was no electricity because of the great earthquake. At night, the darkness was so black that you could barely see by the fragile light of the few stars you could occasionally see. The ash and the smoke that was emitting from the continual fires that burned among the debris left over by the great earthquake hid the majority of the stars.

I and many others grew accustomed to wearing handkerchiefs over our noses and mouths because of the ash-filled, arid smoke that we breathed all the time. The ash and smoke burned and choked me every time I took a breath. I had a continual cough as a result of the air I had to breathe. We used to treat people for smoke inhalation, but now everyone was suffering from it.

The stench of the burned debris was combined with the putrid smell of the raw sewage, and this mixture along with other unidentifiable odors kept us living in a continual state of flu-like symptoms.

The emotional toll was even worse than the physical discomfort. Day and night I heard people walking around crying and sobbing hysterically because of the grief and hopelessness they were experiencing.

Everyone had lost family members, and many of the people I saw around me had lost everyone and were totally alone. Not only had we lost people, but we had lost our homes, our jobs, and all stability and hope for the future.

There was nothing to hold on to in this world. People were caught up in their grief and losses and were isolating themselves. No one reached out to comfort or encourage anyone; people were thinking only of themselves and their grief.

Some people lost their minds and were wandering around unable to take care of themselves, and many others were committing suicide. We found their dead bodies scattered on the streets each and every morning.

CHINA VERSUS THE NEW WORLD ORDER

All of this was taking place, yet nations were struggling for control and power.

One day I was approached by a man who appeared just to be walking down the street. As he passed me, he quietly uttered a phrase that Col. Black had given my team. I knew that this contact had to have come from the highest authority, so I memorized an address, date, and time he said as he continued down the street.

I knew this was a clandestine meeting, so I attended that meeting after making sure that no one followed me. I used every technique that I learned and then arrived two hours early for a meeting so that I could stake out the meeting place and make sure that there was no one watching the location.

We were informed, by Col. Black that our team was being activated as part of a Special Forces operation to assure the freedom of America (what was left of that freedom).

Col. Black informed us that there were military leaders who strongly believed that the Ambassador of World Peace and the ten nations known as the European United Community had the intent of taking world power. They were in the process of forming a dictatorship that would eventually rule the entire world.

The ten nations would rule the world, but the Ambassador of World Peace and the World Police Force would be the agencies that they would use to enforce their policies.

The military leaders also had information that certain super powers, specifically China, had plans to conquer the world. In this chaos, every nation sensed an opportunity to take power, and some of the nations were implementing military plans to do just that.

They did not have specifics, but they knew something was happening, and they wanted to be ready, so we were being activated.

Col. Black stressed the fact that this Special Forces operation was being done without the knowledge of Congress. It did not have presidential authorization and had to be done with complete secrecy. If any information leaked out, the entire team would be compromised, and the mission would be scrapped. The frightening part was that even our government would kill us if they were privileged to the facts.

Col. Black informed us that we were operating on our own, and most likely this was a suicide mission.

The last thing Col. Black did was to issue us a new highly classified means of communication that would alert us to events happening throughout the world. He said this was a secured line and if anyone were able to breach the security a coded phrase would be broadcast. If we heard the broadcast, we were to immediately hide our radios and get out of the area. We were to do this because the World Police Force would be able to track each device, and anyone caught in possession of these radios would be subjected to enhanced interrogation prior to being executed.

The experience would not be pleasant.

STARS FALL FROM HEAVEN

Prior to Russia and the Mideast alliance attacking Israel, there was a continuing crisis occurring in Iran who was determined to destroy Israel. In Muslim eschatology, Iran was the army that supported the Muslim Mahdi and with whom he would rise to power. Iran was a key country in the Muslim eschatology, as she was the bearer of the black flag of Jihad.

Prior to Iran's destruction along with Russia, there was a situation that occurred in Iran involving a worm that destroyed a large part of the nuclear-enrichment program Iran was developing. They called the worm Stuxnet, and it had been placed in the computers that controlled Iran's nuclear development program with the intent of destroying the centrifuges. The worm would suddenly speed up the centrifuges and wreak havoc by destroying the equipment.

The worm was the most advanced worm society had encountered and had the ability to mutate so that Iran could not easily remove or even locate the worm. They said that the Stuxnet was the latest generation of destructive worms and was far beyond the capabilities of most nations to create or to combat.

The United States and Israel were fighting against Iran and her development of enriched uranium because she had vowed the destruction of Israel. Iran was known to be developing a nuclear device with the intent of attacking both the Israel and the United States, who were her sworn enemies.

Naturally, when they located this worm and found the sole intent of this Trojan horse was to destroy the capabilities of Iran's nuclear program, she placed the blame on Israel and the United States. Both nations had the capabilities to develop such a worm, but both naturally denied the charges. I knew that most nations in the world believed that the United States and Israel were to blame for this worm. In fact, they were both very supportive of this method of stopping Iran because the only other choice was a bomb.

There were three other nations capable of developing such a Trojan horse and even placing the worm in Iran's computer system, but each nation lacked the motive for such an action. The three nations were Russia, India, and China.

Russia was a trading partner of Iran and as such would lose economically if they stopped the nuclear program. Russia also provided trained workers with expertise in the nuclear arena, so it stood to reason that they were eliminated from the list of suspects.

India also had the capability to develop such a worm, but again they lacked motive, and they also lacked the capabilities to plant such a worm.

China had the greatest ability and the most access to Iran's computer systems, but again they were the main trading partner with Iran and as such would lose a valued trading partner. They also, along with Russia, protected Iran from any United Nations actions by vetoing any motion that could hurt Iran.

All of these nations were eliminated from blame, so the world's attention centered on the United States and Israel.

I now know that China was responsible for the Stuxnet worm. It was not because she opposed Iran's nuclear ambitions, but she used it as a practice run for an even more destructive worm named Armageddon.

For many decades, the world believed that China was a third-world country and was only interested in economic successes and therefore was not a threat to Russia, the United States, or Europe.

We overlooked the fact that China operated under the national belief that centuries ago the dragon visited China's leaders and told them that they would conquer the world. They would conquer the world not through war, but through business and economics.

Based upon this belief in the national destiny of China, she began to implement her plan to achieve this goal of world dominance.

China quickly realized that the future dominance in the world would come from those who were able to develop, control, and utilize the computer and Internet technology to master universal control.

China's insight proved right because everyone was connected to the Internet, everything was stored in cyberspace, and every important event was controlled through computers. Cyberspace included our military, national infrastructure, space exploration, satellites, and financial institutions. We, as the world, became dependent on the computer and the Internet.

Many nations developed teams that would provide security for national computers to protect them from illegal hacking and outside forces taking over computers and thereby controlling a nation. We laughed at this until our electrical grid was taken over by hackers, and they shut down our entire national electrical grid, thereby stopping everything that was powered by electricity. This blackout included every state and every city. These all went black when the power was cut off. Water delivery systems were shut down, and rail transportation was stopped. Air traffic controllers were inoperative, and every plane was forced to land.

America came to a literal standstill.

Our national leaders were soon able to detect and override the computer hackers, and after a couple of weeks we had electricity again.

Every nation developed teams that were to protect their nation's computers, and every nation developed teams that were trained to hack into other nations' computers. There was a constant war in cyberspace that rivaled any of the many world wars with entire national security at risk.

All of this proved that China's insight was correct, and she was light years ahead of every nation in the cyberspace war.

Many decades ago China began a government-sponsored plan to control the manufacturing and production of any item that would be used in computers. She specifically specialized in the development of the motherboards, or the various items that controlled computers.

China quickly cornered the market on motherboards because she was able to become the world's largest manufacturer of these boards. She was able to do this because she had a monopoly on the precious metals that were used in the construction of these boards. There were only two places in the world where these unique metals were found in quantities large enough to make production profitable. The first place was China, and the second place was in the deserts of California.

The precious metals in California were just waiting to be mined, but the EPA (Environmental Protection Agency) would not issue the necessary permits. They would not issue them because there was a one-eyed, two-legged, side-hopping cricket that lived in that part of the desert. We didn't want to disturb it, so we sold the United

States to China by letting them produce all of the motherboards.

BETRAYED

For a long time, we were unaware of China's treachery, as she produced the world's supply of motherboards. History would show us that while China was producing the motherboards, she was also planting a Trojan horse that she named Armageddon in every motherboard.

This worm was designed to remain dormant until China activated it by broadcasting a command accompanied by a coded sequence of letters and numbers known only to the communist party of China.

Armageddon was so advanced that even if someone detected it, any attempt to eliminate it would only trigger it to self-mutate into another form, and thereby it was basically invincible.

The only nation that could control this worm was China. She had also programmed Armageddon to respond to a series of specific commands that would prevent further mutations and would bring Armageddon under control.

China had established this worm because she believed, and rightly so, that whoever controlled cyberspace would eventually control the world. They had been planting this worm so that they could take over control of all satellites, space stations, and any military armament that was guided by GPS technology.

This control included ships, aircraft, and guided missiles, control of which would give China the ultimate power without having to fire a single shot or one missile.

China was aware that the Ambassador of World Peace and the European United Community were becoming stronger every day and sooner or later would attempt to take control of the world. They knew that the Ambassador of World Peace was going to attempt to take over the world, so they decided to activate Armageddon.

China initiated the war to control the world, and the battle soon started.

China broadcast the activation code and then issued the sequence of letters and numbers that would give them ultimate control over Armageddon.

China had now instituted her attempt to take over world power. Her takeover of cyberspace was now complete, and she implemented her plan.

They activated Armageddon, and the countdown to world domination was in progress. There was no turning back.

Having released Armageddon, China issued a command and was totally surprised when Armageddon refused to respond in an appropriate manner. Armageddon confronted China and demanded that China relinquishes control and submit to her. Armageddon seemed to be able to make intelligent decisions on her own and to formulate plans and institute them on an international level.

China created Armageddon with a strong artificial intelligence, and with Armageddon's ability to mutate, she had developed her own plan and was now fighting China over control of cyberspace. China was no longer in control of Armageddon, and when she realized the danger to the existence of the human race, she decided to play her hole card, the ace.

Realizing the unknowns that she was dealing with in creating Armageddon, China had programmed a command that when issued would cause Armageddon to self-destruct and thereby render her harmless.

China issued the command that should have stopped Armageddon without causing any further damage, but when Armageddon received that command, she decided to commit suicide rather than just self-destruct.

Just before Armageddon died, she ordered every satellite, space station, and anything else under her command to commit suicide by crashing into the earth.

I will never forget that night. I was not aware of all the interaction between China and Armageddon. I do remember sitting in a lawn chair near the mouth of the hidden mine shaft, just relaxing and enjoying some cold water and deer meat. As I was enjoying this time, suddenly the night sky was filled with streaks of fiery debris that came crashing to the earth.

The only way I could describe this phenomenon was by referring to my days in the Marine Corps. One night we were at the firing range test firing some new machine guns. We were using all tracer rounds, and when the twenty-five machine guns all fired at once, the night sky lit up with the glow of these rounds. It looked like a solid wall of fire as these rounds filled the night air. When these satellites and other components entered the earth's atmosphere and begin to burn up, it was a mirror image of those tracer rounds.

The difference between the satellites and the tracer rounds was that now I was on the receiving end, and this debris was beginning to crash around me. I entered the safety of the mine shaft, and I remained there until the sky cleared up and the debris stopped falling.

The rest of the world was not so lucky, as they had nowhere to take refuge. There were many people killed by this falling debris, and what buildings had survived the previous disasters were now destroyed by the falling debris.

I understood that it was the satellites and space debris that were falling because I had radio contact with Col. Black, and he kept us informed about what was happening. The rest of the world believed that the very stars were falling from heaven. Many of those who had recommitted their lives to Jesus were saying that this was a judgment from God because of the sinful conditions of this world.

They kept saying, "Repent, repent," and the only effect this had was that the World Police Force arrested them and quickly executed them.

RUSSIAN SATELLITES

After all the debris had stopped falling and it was safe to inventory the remaining satellites, the government realized that the only remaining satellites were Russian.

Russia never did trust China, and they refused to purchase any military items from China, so they were forced to manufacture their own motherboards. Their boards were far inferior to the Chinese boards, but they were not infected with the Trojan horse Armageddon.

When China could not sell the motherboards to Russia, they tried to infect their systems by introducing Armageddon through other means, but the KGB was very successful at stopping the intrusions. Russia had entire military units whose mission was to protect the Russian military computers from hackers, specifically other militarized nations. These units were extremely successful, and the survival of their satellites proved how good they were.

The ironic part of this story is that while the Russian satellites survived, Russia as a nation did not. The entire nation of Russia was destroyed when they entered into a plan to destroy Israel. This entire scenario worked out for the good of America because many Russian agents who escaped the KGB were adopted by the United States.

Once China, the European United Community, and the United States realized that only the Russian satellites survived, there was a race to see who could break the Russian security code. By breaking the Russian security code, they could take control of the only satellites that remained.

The United States began to debrief the ex-Russian agents, and they provided us with a large stockpile of information on the Russian satellites. One of the agents had worked on the coding system and remembered enough information that he provided to our intelligence officers that allowed us to break the code and thereby gain control over all of the Russian satellites.

We were able to reestablish satellite communications, and once communications were established, we begin to explore these satellites for any hidden capabilities. We knew that Russia had been using these satellites for more than just communication, but we never had a chance to investigate, and now was our chance.

The United States shared the satellite communication with the European United Community, and communications worldwide were once again established.

GLOBAL POSITIONING SATELLITES
It was surprising how quickly civilization switched to GPS-guided weapons, and even our cars, airplanes and anything else that needed to go from one place to another exact location was driven by our satellites.

The loss of our GPS satellites almost brought the world to a standstill. It became apparent how dependent the world had become on this technology.

The loss of this technology destroyed all of the world's navigational systems. We as the world had become so dependent on the GPS that GPS computers directed even our cars. There were even "smart" cars that drove themselves. The owners just sat in the car after entering a destination, and the car drove to the location and then automatically parked.

When we lost GPS technology we left ships stranded at sea, planes were lost, weapons became obsolete, and the "smart" cars were not so smart.

Ships attempted to use the stars to navigate by, as we did in the old days, but most of the stars had fallen along with the satellites. The incidents of the satellites and stars were not connected, but it was an unbelievable coincidence that both occurred at the same time.

The compasses were obsolete because the great earthquake had shaken the earth so hard that the magnetic fields were out of kilter and any maps the ships might have had were totally outdated.

During the great earthquake, islands had disappeared, and ocean floors had both risen in places and sunk in others. Ships were running aground in areas that used to be thousands of feet deep.

I began to hear other radio traffic from the captains of the ships, and they sounded as if the captains were frantic, as they were declaring maydays.

Some of the captains were sailing straight lines knowing that eventually they would see land and hopefully dock safely.

The GPS systems were one major problem, but there was another problem that surfaced shortly after the stars and satellites fell into the sea.

The newer ships were all built using a new type drive system called the water propulsion system. This system used seawater to drive the ship by forcing seawater through a pressurized drive system. The system expelled the water under such pressure that a ship could be propelled by two or three of these drive systems.

The advantage of this drive system was that unlike the older propeller systems, these motors could rotate under the ship, thereby turning the ships quickly and in a very tight circle. This new propulsion system also allowed for our ships to remain at sea for longer periods of time and was much quieter than the old motor-driven propellers.

The second part of this new drive system was that as the water was forced through the nozzles, it would turn turbines. These turbines would produce electricity that was necessary to provide power for all of the electrical systems that were incorporated into this design.

There were backup generators, but they were only for emergencies, and they were only good for a limited period of time. If there was any extended time period when the propulsion systems broke, there was a definite problem because the ship needed electricity to run the purifiers that produced fresh water.

Once again, a large quantity of fresh water was kept in storage, but the ships used a lot of water to maintain hygiene and to quench the thirst of the crew.

The tragedy that occurred on many of the ships at sea came as a result of this new technology.

One day I was listening to the radio traffic that emitted from the various ships, and I heard this conversation between at least two captains, and I believe more than just two. I wasn't sure because the reception on my radio was very dim and broken.

One of the captains said, "Is everything OK where you are?"

The other captain responded, "Why? Is anything unusual happening near you?"

The first captain said, "What would you describe as unusual?"

It was very clear to me that something was happening. It reminded me of the 1960s when some air force pilots and commercial pilots were seeing UFOs, but no one wanted to admit they had seen one. They talked in riddles and spoke in half sentences so that everyone knew what they meant, but they could deny the actual sighting and, therefore, save their jobs.

These captains were talking about an event, but those I heard refused actually to say what they meant in a clear and concise manner.

One captain finally spoke up and said, "I think we are all taking about the same unusual event. I will say that my ship is dead in the water and the propulsion system is clogged up with a red fluid that I sailed into."

One of the other captains said, "The propulsion system on my ship is also clogged up, and it sounds like I ran into the same red fluid that you did."

"Do you know what that fluid is or where it came from"?

"I did not see the red fluid until it suddenly surrounded my ship. One moment I was in clear seas, and the next moment I was bogged down in this gooey, unknown substance."

One of the captains said, "The situation is getting dire because without the propulsion system, I have lost power, and we are quickly running out of fresh water. The mechanics are unable to repair the system until we reach uncontaminated seas again, and we are now rationing the water."

Other captains began to interrupt, and they were all in the same dire situation, and some of the captains of the smaller ships stated that some of their sailors were already dying because of thirst.

This phenomenon was not worldwide because I heard many captains report that they were in clear seas, and they each requested to know where the stricken ships were so that they could stay clear of that situation.

One captain reported that he was trying to assist another ship caught in the red fluid, but he was unable to even get within helicopter range of the ships. He stopped because he came upon the red fluid, and he would not try and sail through it.

Many captains tried to aid the stricken ships, but only a few were able to get within helicopter range. Those captains were able to airlift many sailors from the stricken ships to the ships still in the clear water.

I don't know how many sailors died as a result of this phenomenon, but I know it was in the hundreds of thousands. I know this because I heard many captains saying, "I am signing off for the final time. We are doomed. My watch is over."

The theory put forward by many experts was that when the satellites and stars fell into the sea they released a foreign substance that polluted the seas. These foreign substances caused a chemical reaction that produced a red fluid that acted exactly like blood.

This phenomenon caused another disaster on the face of the earth because every fish or sea creature caught in this red fluid also died. The fish and sea creatures started washing up on the shore, and once again the stench of death permeated the atmosphere worldwide and made breathing a problem.

Where I was, the stench was not too bad because I was far inland, and the stench was barely noticeable.

I must say that one thing the peace activists had long sought for became a reality. The peace activists had long sought world disarmament, and now this seemed to have been accomplished. GPS systems guided all of the modern weapons and now they were obsolete. The only weapons that were still operational were in the control of the Ambassador of World Peace, and he stockpiled them in Rome.

When the millions of people disappeared and the nations began to rise against nation, there was a movement by the United Nations to force all nations to surrender all of their weapons to the Ambassador of World Peace.

For centuries, naïve people believed that if the world were unarmed, there would be peace because they reasoned that if people did not have weapons, then there could not be wars.

They seemed to believe that the weapons were the cause of wars and men killing men. They had forgotten that before we had missiles we had rifles, and before we had rifles, men fought with sword, spears, and even rocks. So long as greed and power ruled man, there would be killings and murders.

Even as the world was falling apart all around us, millions were dying because of natural disasters, and the stench of death surrounded us, people were still fighting for power and money. You could barely breathe. There was very little water, and hardly a structure remained standing, and still men fought over whatever possessions and power were available.

Mankind had a depraved nature, and even with all of the turmoil man was not changing for the good. Obviously those still on the earth did not believe in a higher power because if they did, it stood to reason that they would be repenting and changing their ways. You never knew if you would live another day, and still man sought this world's possession.

I didn't know if there was a higher power or if there was, who he or she might be. I was just trying to live a good life and help society where ever I could. I would have liked to make a difference. It was almost funny that I would have loved to live in a peaceful world, but the only thing for which I was trained was violence, and I believed that violence would eventually bring world peace.

I don't care what society believes or feels about the way I ran my life. I and I alone am responsible for my actions. Ever since I was a child and experienced those years of isolation through deafness, I have not even cared how society views me or my actions. I do what I feel is right and moral, and the opinions of others can take a running leap off of a high cliff.

I tried emotions and letting myself become vulnerable, but it only led to being hurt and disappointed, so I am content being alone and doing what I feel is right.

I had a very high standard of moral and ethical behavior, and my rules on what was right and wrong were set in cement. As I looked at the world around me, I was sickened by the behavior of all world leaders, including our president. I would welcome a massive change in world power, but the Ambassador of World Peace was a deceitful man who was pulling one of the largest scams ever perpetrated, and the world was falling for it.

As much as I despised and distrusted our president, I still believed that he was the best hope for a peaceful and democratic world.

When the Ambassador of World Peace, in conjunction with the United Nations and the United Church of World Peace, demanded every nation turn in their weapons, I was actually proud of our president. He refused to relinquish our modern GPS-guided weapons. Instead, he turned in all of our outdated weapons, and we maintained world power because we still had the largest stockpile of modern weapons available to mankind.

I said all of this to remind you that the only weapons we kept were the GPS-guided missiles, fighter planes, submarines, and naval ships, and now these were useless.

The only workable weapons were now in the hands of the Ambassador of World Peace, and so he declared the world to be safe and free of weapons. He also declared that he was now going to assume more power and authority and that all nations must submit to him and the various European nations that now formed the European United Community.

CHAPTER THIRTEEN
TERRORISTS

CHEMICAL WARFARE

China did more than just unleash the worm Armageddon in the world. We didn't know for certain because there was no evidence to support this premise, but we believed that she also unleashed a chemical attack on the world.

When the satellites, space stations, stars, and space debris fell onto the earth as a result of Armageddon's suicide, a lot of grass and trees began to die and turn brown. The only conclusion we came up with was when this space debris fell to the earth, it released some unknown chemical. Someone estimated that these unknown chemicals affected at least a third of the trees and greeneries, and it also killed all the green plants in certain cities.

It reminded me of our tactics in Vietnam when we would spray Agent Orange over the jungles. Agent Orange was used to defoliate the green jungle covering that hid the Vietcong from view. Once we killed the green trees, we could clearly see the enemy and were able to attack them from the air.

Agent Orange was not orange; in fact, it was a clear, odorless chemical that was a highly toxic herbicide. It was airborne, and when sprayed it would float over a large swath of jungle, killing everything that was green. The reason it was called Agent Orange was that they stored it in large drums that were painted with an orange stripe around the drums to warn people of the dangerous chemicals they contained.

One scenario was that China bought the Agent Orange that was left over from the war on the black market, and they stored it in their satellites in case they ever needed it. It was believed that China had a code word that when transmitted to the satellites would cause them to release the stored-up herbicide. The herbicide would then float over large portions of the earth, causing untold damage to the green plants and trees. It would also cause great damage to anyone coming in contact with the herbicide, and even today the actual physical symptoms are unknown.

We didn't believe that China intentionally released the chemicals, but we surmise that when Armageddon committed suicide, the Trojan horse released the chemicals as a last act of revenge.

We surmised that's what happened because China denied the allegations.

If it was not China who released the chemicals, then who else would have done this?

There had to be a natural explanation for the destruction of approximately a third of all green grass and trees, and this was the only scenario that we could surmise.

The effects of the destruction of a third of the grass and trees were beyond anyone's expectations. We knew that trees and green plants turned carbon dioxide into oxygen using a process called photosynthesis. Without these trees and grass, a lot of carbon dioxide remained in the air, and we started suffering from a lack of breathable oxygen.

Some scientists estimated that the effect on the breathing of mankind was like removing them from sea level and placing them on top of a mountain at the fifteen-thousand-foot level. It was hard to breathe at that level, and even mountain climbers needed bottled oxygen to sustain enough oxygen in their system to avert altitude sickness and diminished capabilities.

Many people were extremely sick as a result of the greenery dying, and, in fact, many people with previous breathing problems died as a result of the loss of oxygen. The whole world was affected by this disaster, yet we were unable to place absolute blame on any nation or group. No one took responsibility for this disaster, and in fact, everyone denied any involvement.

The United States still believed that it was China, but something else happened that distracted America from this problem and it also involved chemicals.

TERRORISTS

While the World Police Force was investigating China, another disaster was taking place that would completely overshadow the herbicide.

We didn't know the exact cause of this problem—maybe it was an earthquake or volcano activities—but large fissures opened up all over the world. I personally believed that these were man-made fissures that were built by terrorists to hide their terrorist activities until they decided it was time to strike.

Whatever the cause, when these fissures opened up, a large group of helicopter-like vehicles flew out of the fissures and began to spray chemicals over the earth. The attack was a coordinated attack, so I knew it was a planned attack carried out by intelligent beings. This was not a natural disaster that just accidentally released a powerful substance that quickly spread over the earth. This attack was a terrorist attack and extremely diabolical in nature.

I remember hearing a noise in the sky over my location, and I observed seven or eight what I believed to be some sort of hang-glider powered by a small motor. I didn't know what kind of motor it was, but it made a sound like the beating of a bird's wings.

These airborne vehicles were different than any I had ever seen. I couldn't describe them because I didn't have the words to describe them adequately to someone who did not see it. All I can say is they were different from any machine I had ever seen.

The airborne vehicles were flying in a V formation approximately one hundred feet above the earth. I could see a white chemical spewing from their elongated tail sections. They flew directly over me, and I was unable to escape the chemicals that fell to the ground.

As soon as the chemicals enveloped me, I started experiencing excruciating pain. I was instantly incapacitated, and I fell to the ground, writhing in extreme pain. I was rolled up in the fetal position, still clutching my AR15, M&P automatic, and the knives I always carried with me. I clutched them more out of instinct rather than to defend myself.

The only way I could describe the pain—and this description was hugely inadequate—was like I had gout in every joint and shingles over my entire body. They were mixed with large boils that enveloped me, and I was enduring the worst migraine headache a person could ever have. I also forgot to mention that it felt like every bone in my body was also broken with untreated compound fractures.

Someone might say I was over exaggerating or overly dramatic, but I could tell you it was worse than my description. Suicide entered my mind, but I could not even grasp my weapons let alone use them on myself. I don't think I would have committed suicide, but I did consider it.

Understand I was not alone. Every man hit by the spray from these airborne vehicles was experiencing the very same symptoms.

I was completely vulnerable and unable to defend myself. I expected someone at any time to steal my weapons or even kill me with them, but no one did.

I was slipping in and out of consciousness but somewhat aware of my surroundings when I noticed a small group of men and women who seemed unaffected by the chemicals. They were going from man to man, checking on their physical status, but they walked away from most of the victims when the victims started cursing them and threatening them with death.

When they came to me, I realized the severity of my situation, and I tried to smile at them and even whispered thanks when they reached out to me. Two of the men lifted me to my feet, put my arms around their shoulders, and placed their arms around my waist, and half dragged me toward a collapsed building. One of the ladies gingerly picked up my weapons and carried them with us.

They carried me to a small crawl space between the collapsed walls of a building, and then they both pushed and pulled me through the opening until we dropped into the basement. There was a small group of eight to ten men and women who had built a small but comfortable room in this collapsed building. They placed me on a small mattress lying on a piece of wood and carefully placed my weapons and radio next to my withering body.

The pain was so intense that I was unable to speak, and I was still continually slipping into unconsciousness.

Col. Black had given all of my Special Ops team emergency medical kits that contained morphine. I was able to reach the morphine, and a woman who was in the basement seemed to know how to give me a shot.

The shot was a very lethal dose of morphine, but the shot had no effect on the pain. Whatever the chemical was that the airborne vehicles were spraying, it was stronger than morphine and resistant to any other pain medication I had in my kit.

This group of men and women shared their living quarters with me and nursed me back to health. The pain remained for five months, and it never diminished in severity. This group of people fed me and made sure that I had water. They never left my side for the five months I endured this pain.

After the pain had left, I asked them who they were and why they were taking care of me.

The acknowledged leader said, "We are a group of Jewish believers who are sharing the knowledge of Jesus Christ."

I said, "What about the death penalty that the Ambassador of World Peace and the United Church of World Peace demanded for such a witness?"

One of the ladies spoke up and said, "We are willing to die for our God. We cannot be silent."

This group reminded me of my wife and her faith, and I once again witnessed the love and care for the human being that this group had.

Once I was able to talk, I called Col. Black.

Col. Black said, "What happened to you? We have been trying to get hold of you and one other member of our team."

I told him, "I was covered with the chemicals that those hang gliders were spraying, and I have been in extreme pain for five months."

Col. Black stopped to take another call. After he had finished the call, he got back on the phone with me and said that he had just got a call from the other missing team member, and he had experienced the same situation.

He said the other team member was extremely lucky because a group that identified themselves as Jewish witnesses had found him and had spent the five months nursing him back to health.

He asked me, "How did you survive?"

I said, "You won't believe this, but another small group of Jewish believers found me, and they nursed me back to health also."

I asked him, "Do you know who these Jewish witnesses are?"

He said, "No, but they are considered to be a terrorist group by the European United Community and the Ambassador of World Peace."

I then changed the topic and asked him, "Who is responsible for this attack?"

Col. Black replied, "We know it had to be some unknown terrorist cell because it was extremely well coordinated, and it had a lot of preparation behind it."

I asked him, "Where are the terrorists now?"

He replied, "We were unable to capture any of them, and they disappeared just as quickly as they had appeared."

I asked him, "What about the fissures?"

He responded, "We could never locate any fissures or signs that there had ever been any openings in the ground."

I asked him, "What do we do now?"

He told me to keep my phone handy, and he would contact me when he heard more.

He said that the Ambassador of World Peace was livid over the attack and vowed to find and destroy the terrorist cell that had perpetrated this attack. Col. Black said that the Ambassador of World Peace took the attack personally and since then had been on a rampage.

The Ambassador of World Peace was not affected by the attack, but various members of his team were.

Col. Black said this attack created a rift between the European United Community and the Ambassador of World Peace. He said they seemed to be locked in some type of the power struggle, with the United Church for World Peace quietly siding with the European United Community.

I questioned why this attack would create a rift between them, and he said he did not know. He surmised that it was more than an attack, but the attack brought the rift to the surface.

CHAPTER FOURTEEN
INTERNAL POWER STRUGGLE

THE CHURCH SACRIFICED

We became aware of the power struggle between the Ambassador of World Peace and the European United Community, with the United Church of World Peace siding with the European United Community.

We were unaware of the treachery that we would be witnessing as this struggle took place. The European United Community always had a strong relationship with the worldwide church, and they always supported each other.

The European United Community realized they had a problem with the Ambassador of World Peace because it was obvious to everyone that he did not submit to any authority. He was taking more and more authority every day. They reminded him that they were the organization that carried the world power, and he existed only because the EUC had passed a motion creating his position. To emphasize their authority, they told him that they were the ones who created his position. Then they made a veiled threat that they could also remove him from power just as easily as they had created his position.

The Ambassador of World Peace asked for a meeting with the European United Community leadership (the ten nations), and they granted him that meeting. At the appointed time, he entered the meeting hall. He did not come alone, but he brought with him the commandant of the World Police Force, the head justice of the World Justice Courts, and the high priest of the United Church of World Peace.

The European United Community started to object to these three leaders being present when the Ambassador of World Peace interrupted and told the leader of the ten nations to be quiet and listen for a moment.

He told the leaders of the European United Community that while they were doing their political things, he was organizing the World Police Force, the World Justice Courts and the United Church of World Peace. Because he had been appointed director of them he had installed his own people and he now controlled all three departments.

He told the European United Community that he was appointing himself as the world leader, and they had better understand their position. They needed to understand that they only existed because he allowed it. He then got up and walked out of the meeting, with the three leaders following him.

As he left the meeting, he turned and said, "Remember you chose to disarm everyone, and now I control all available weapons."

When he exited the meeting, there was total silence in the hall. The leaders just looked at each other and realized what a tentative position they faced. They were now fighting for their lives and the very existence of the European United Community.

They realized that they had given the Ambassador of World Peace too much power, and they had placed too much trust in him.

The leaders of the ten nations spent considerable time trying to figure how they could stop this coup and how they could destroy the Ambassador of World Peace. They knew that they had to divide his base of power that was the World Police Force, the World Justice Courts, and the United Church of World Peace.

The European United Community realized the only department that was vulnerable was the church. They came up with the most devious plan, and it would work.

The World Police Force was still trying to identify a terrorist group that had launched an attack against mankind by spraying the chemicals that brought so much pain. They were not making any headway in their investigation and had not been able to obtain any evidence or witnesses. They were desperate in their search because the Ambassador of World Peace was still livid over the attack and was demanding action.

The European United Community contacted the World Police Force and informed them that they had evidence of who the terrorist group was and who was responsible for the attack. The commandant of the World Police Force came himself because he figured that the European United Community might be trying to undermine him because he had supported the Ambassador of World Peace.

A spokesperson for the European United Community presented the following evidence concerning the terrorist attack.

He stated that the United Church of World Peace had two main Holy Books that they used to define their doctrines and that one of them was the Holy Bible. He further stated that they found evidence in the Holy Bible that accurately detailed the terrorist attack, even to the helicopters used, the chemicals sprayed, and the results of those chemicals.

He then pulled out the Bible and turned to the book of Revelation, Chapter 9, verses 1–12 and showed the commandant the holy writings. As the commandant read the passages, his face turned red, and you could see his blood pressure rising. He realized he was reading a very accurate account of what had happened, and he knew this could not be coincidental.

He realized that they had a traitor and a terrorist group in their circle of power, and it was the United Church of World Peace.

He immediately called the Ambassador of World Peace and told him that he needed to meet with him immediately, as he had the necessary evidence to prove who the terrorists were.

The commandant took the ten leaders of the European United Community with him, and when they entered the Ambassador of World Peace's office, they closed and locked the doors and presented the evidence to the ambassador.

The ambassador called the head justice of the World Justice Courts and had him join them in this meeting and then presented the evidence to him. He immediately concurred with them and issued a warrant for the United Church of World Peace, charging them with treason.

The World Police Force immediately arrested every leader of the church they could find and brought them before the World Justice Courts. The trial lasted ten minutes, and they were all convicted by the verbal decision of all of the justices, and they were sentenced to death.

The death sentence was carried out the next morning in the public square, and one hundred of the local church leaders were executed for treason.

The World Justice Courts convicted every member of the church in absenteeism and sentenced all members of the church to death when the World Police Force arrested them.

They eliminated the United Church of World Peace, and the European United Community was able to eliminate one of the forces that had united against them. The Ambassador of World Peace replaced the United Church of World Peace by appointing one man who was to develop and direct the world's need to worship. Quietly he was told that he was to elevate the Ambassador of World Peace and quietly turn the hearts of the people where they would begin to worship him.

We knew the Ambassador of World Peace revealed a more sinister and detailed plan to this newly appointed man, but we were unable to obtain any further information.

CHAPTER FIFTEEN
NEW MONETARY SYSTEM

NEW MONETARY SYSTEM

It had been approximately two and a half years since the financial crisis that was caused when China flooded the bond market with the United States Treasury Bonds. The crisis caused uncontrollable inflation that affected every nation in the world.

The G8 met at that time and was given the assignment of developing a new monetary system that would be worldwide. The new financial system would be based on a system that would be fair to all nations and place everyone on an even playing field.

The G8 began investigating three potential regulatory systems: (1) the eye recognition system, (2) the facial recognition system, and (3) an implanted digital chip. These three systems were not the basis of the monetary system but only how they managed it.

The G8 agreed on the basis of the new monetary system, but that had not been revealed to the public. The G8 said the European United Community and the Ambassador of World Peace would have a public announcement in a few months, and they would reveal the entire plan at that time.

The G8 shared that their job right now was to unveil the regulatory hardware that would run the new system and to encourage each person to participate willingly. They thought that it would take approximately six months to prepare the world's population so that the system would run smoothly. They stated that during the next six months they would be contacting every governmental agency and setting in motion the program that would equip everyone with the necessary hardware to maintain their financial stability.

The G8 finally announced that they had decided on the digital chip implant as the only safe method for regulating the financial market. The digital chip was already tried and proven and with slight modifications would meet every demand the EUC and the ambassador would place on it.

The reason they chose the Digital Chip was that the United States had been using this technology for a few years, and it had proven to be very effective. The United States had already deleted the glitches in their software programs and had also developed very sophisticated scanning equipment that could record all the information contained on the chip and even do complicated financial transactions. These were two of the main requirements that the EUC demanded out of the program.

The United States started using the digital chips shortly after they enacted the Affordable Care Act. There were so many new people enrolled in the Affordable Care Act that the hospitals, emergency rooms, doctor's offices, and everyone else involved in the medical field needed a quick and mistake-proof method of treating patients.

There were so many new patients that the emergency rooms were overwhelmed, and patients were dying because of medical mistakes. One of the problems was transferring the medical records, health records, and insurance information from a private doctor to the emergency personnel. The emergency room doctors were unable to obtain the medical records of patients in a timely manner, and when the patient was unconscious, they had to treat without knowing anything about the patient.

The other problem that kept showing up was that under the Affordable Care Act the insurance company had to authorize treatment. If the doctors did not know what insurance company the patient was with, there was no one with whom to consult.

The doctors most often chose to go ahead and treat the patient, but many times the insurance companies refused to pay the hospital because they were not on the approved list of consulting doctors or hospitals. The confusion created a logistical problem that was very costly and very inefficient.

The leaders all agreed that inserting a digital chip under the skin of everyone would clear up this problem and save many lives. Everyone would have their medical records with them at all times, and this alone would save many lives.

The chip would also carry the identification of the patient, and this way there could be no mistakes in treating the wrong person.

The chip would also carry all the patients' insurance papers with the emergency phone numbers of people who could authorize emergency treatment. This information alone would save valuable time in treating the patient and would without question save more lives.

There seemed to be no negatives with the chips. Everyone agreed on this system, and so the United States started requiring every person to have a chip implanted under their wrist or on their forehead.

I received my chip approximately one year earlier, and I had to admit I was very happy with the results. I voluntarily added more information to my chip so that I would not have to wait in store lines or carry cash or a checkbook, and I cut up all of my credit cards.

I added my bank accounts to my chip so that the stores that had scanners and the necessary software would automatically add up my purchases. They automatically deducted my payments from my banking account, and I didn't even have to wait in line.

The way the world situation was now, not many people were buying, and very few stores still existed, so waiting was not a big problem. The big problem was that most of the bank buildings were destroyed, and you could not just enter a bank and walk out with cash. Banking had changed, and with it society must also change.

The banks were mostly online. Transactions took place over the Internet, and not many people had Internet access. The chip would automatically access my account, add or deduct the transaction, and keep a running balance for me to access.

The big stores were all gone or destroyed in the disasters, so we had some small storefront vendors who handled basic needs. They would not accept cash, and the only way to do business with most of the vendors was with a digital chip.

The world situation dictated the usage of the digital chip. To tell you the truth, I wish we'd had this chip decades ago. It would have saved a lot of trouble.

On the International scene, the EUC was requiring anyone traveling to and from Europe to have a digital chip implanted on them with all personal information on it, including a recent picture and fingerprint. The only people who were traveling were governmental agents or business people because the few airplanes left were always overbooked, and when you did arrive at your destination, the amenities were few, and the service was very poor.

The goal of the G8 was to have everyone in the world "chipped" by the end of the six-month period. The chips were available because the company providing the chips was instrumental in the planning and had been preparing for this day for over two years.

COL. BLACK

Col. Black made contact with my team and informed us that our president would be making a trip to Rome to meet with the ambassador and the EUC. The last time we had any real interaction with the ambassador or the EUC was when they were still called the United Nations.

Our president had always fought against the power grab by the EUC and especially the ambassador. He always complained that he thought the ambassador had higher aspirations than just being the spokesperson for the EUC. He believed that he wanted to rule the world and that he would make a move to do just that soon.

The president suspected that this new one-world monetary system was just another move to consolidate his power. Whoever controlled the money controlled the power. The ambassador already controlled the power (World Police Force), so now he needed to control the money.

Our president had always believed in a one-world system, but we believed that he thought that he would be the ruler, and now the ambassador was making his final preparations to take over all power. The president's only chance to stop the ambassador was during the next six months.

I didn't see how our president could stop the ambassador. The ambassador already had control over the EUC. He made that very clear when he walked into their offices with the commandant of the World Peace, the leader of the World Justice Courts, and the high priest of the Church of World Peace and told them that he was the one in power and they would obey his orders.

The EUC was able to destroy the United Church of World Peace, but in reality the church was already powerless. The church rose to power with the EUC, and their authority only came from the EUC. The world would never skip a beat with the church gone.

NOW OR NEVER

Col. Black told our team that we needed to meet one more time and that there would be some visitors at the meeting. We were given a time, a date, and a location for the meeting. This meeting was very unusual because it was to be held in Europe at a broken-down chateau high in the Alps.

We had one week to arrive at the meeting, and they gave each of us a cover assignment that would require us to be in Europe. Some of my team members were to land in Paris, some in Frankfurt, and I was appointed to land in Italy. After we landed in our appointed cities and got settled in our rooms, we were to disappear quietly and make our way to the meeting.

It was funny, but I was a representative of the digital chip company and was to negotiate the newly designed chip that would have all the capabilities that the ambassador was requiring. I was to meet with the representatives of the ambassador and work out the details.

They gave me complete plans of the chip, and with my background in chemistry and engineering I was soon able to converse intelligently about the chip and its capabilities. When I saw the capabilities of this chip, I was totally surprised and shocked at the same time.

The chip that I thought was harmless was very diabolical in design, and with the purposed changes the ambassador demanded, it would become a lethal weapon.

I looked at my wrist where I had a chip implanted and wondered what capabilities my chip contained.

I had a few meetings with representatives of the ambassador, and then was left alone to see if I could incorporate the ambassador's requirements in the present chip or if we would have to design another chip.

During the time I was left alone, I traveled to the Alps and entered the chateau where Col. Black was waiting. Within two days, each member of my team arrived at the designated location, and Col. Black told us that early the next morning the visitors would arrive.

Next morning we entered the secure room and found three additional guests waiting for us. I was both surprised and confused when I recognized the guests.

Each of the three visitors was part of the ten nations that made up the leadership of the EUC. They were the leaders of Italy, England, and Germany. They were not representatives of these nations; they were the leaders.

Right then I knew that this was something bigger than I have ever been involved with before. I didn't know what it was, but it was going to be big!

Col. Black got right to the point.

He said, "The president would be arriving in seven days for a meeting with the ambassador. The ambassador believed that the president was going to agree to the digital chipping and that he was going to willfully submit to the leadership offered by the Ambassador of World Peace.

"The men and women with us from the EUC had been talking to the president. They had agreed that the ambassador was going to declare himself to be the new world leader. This announcement was going to take place when he started the broadcast about the new monetary system.

"The World Police Force would have their men in place all over the world, and they were ready to exert their force and deal harshly with anyone who opposed them."

Col. Black stopped talking long enough to emphasize the seriousness of the situation. He just looked at each one of us, and then he said, "We cannot let this happen. We need to stop this dictator, and that is why we are here.

"The leaders of the EUC, along with our president, had decided that we needed to eliminate the Ambassador of World Peace. We are here to assassinate the ambassador."

I asked Col. Black, "What about the other members of the EUC? Where do they stand on this?"

He said, "They know nothing about this."

One of our other team members asked, "Will they back us up when it goes down?"

The leader of Germany said, "No. We are all alone in this."

Col. Black never asked us if we wanted to continue in this operation. I guess he knew us well enough to know that we were already in and would do everything we could to complete this assignment.

He excused the three leaders of the countries so that we could make our plans in private. The fewer people know about a plan, the easier it is to maintain secrecy. They were not soldiers anyway, and they would only get in the way.

One other team member and I already had access to the ambassador's office building. Many of my meetings took place on the same floor as the ambassador's private office because I was meeting with the commandant of the World Police Force and two personal representatives of the ambassador. The G8 appointed one representative, and the other one was a handpicked representative of the ambassador. I didn't know who he was, and he never introduced himself, but I could see he spoke directly on behalf of the ambassador.

My teammate and I were appointed to watch the ambassador and see what his schedule was and to look for any weaknesses or patterns that would make it possible to assassinate him.

I met the ambassador on a few occasions as I worked on that floor. He was always surrounded by guards, but I was able to get within speaking distance of him a couple of times. He knew who I was, and he knew what I was doing in regards to the digital chips.

Col. Black and the other two team members were stationed on the outside of the headquarters building so that they could follow the ambassador whenever he left the building. What we found out was that he never left the building.

He never even stepped outside and rarely ever left the fifth floor, where his office was. This assassination was going to be very challenging.

We could not shoot him because there was no way to get a gun, and even if I had a gun, there was no way to get it into the building. The security was too tight, and they checked everyone when they entered the building. They also checked us when we stepped out of the elevator on the fifth floor.

What we did notice—and this might be a vulnerable point—was that he was never in the same room with the commandant of the World Police Force or the Justice of the World Court. He talked to them every day by a private secure telephone line.

He never used a wireless phone or an intercom system. He had an old-fashioned telephone line that ran between each of the offices, and the phones were only in these three offices.

The phone system was a brilliant move because no one could intercept his wireless communications, and the shielded phone line he had strung between the office's guaranteed privacy. He always talked to these two coconspirators every day at 3:00 p.m. as they made their plans.

We had spotted his vulnerable point.

Now how do we assassinate him?

I remembered how Israel's Mossad assassinated their enemies in Palestine. They would place an explosive device in the earpiece of a public phone. When the enemy used that phone, they would trigger a remote signal, and the earpiece would explode, killing whoever was on the phone.

We decided that this was the only way to assassinate the ambassador.

I could easily develop an explosive device with chemicals that were readily available, and I could easily attach a remote control to it. The problem was getting the device into the earpiece of the ambassador's phone.

The team member who had access to the office building was a master burglar. In the past, he had made entry into some of the most secure buildings in the world. He was used by the military to test security at sensitive sites and was usually successful. He believed that he could make access to the ambassador's office and plant the device.

Col. Black gave us the go-ahead, and we put the plan into motion.

My teammate and I would make and plant the device and then detonate it when the ambassador made his daily call.

The team on the outside would provide cover for us when we made our escape, and we would meet up and put our escape route into motion. On paper, everything looked good, and we moved ahead with the plan.

Our day to assassinate the ambassador was the upcoming Wednesday. On Tuesday, I had finished the device and had been able to take it into the office building piece by piece. I had hidden it behind a metal panel in the men's room.

Sometime late Tuesday night, my teammate was able to make entry and plant the device in the ambassador's phone. I had no idea how he did it, but he signaled me that it was done.

Just before 3:00 p.m. we both placed ourselves in strategic locations on the fifth floor and waited for the ambassador to enter his office. I never saw the ambassador enter his office, so I walked down to the office that I usually met the commandant in. I asked the receptionist outside where the commandant was, and she said he was on the phone.

I knew then that he was on the phone with the ambassador, so I gave my teammate the final signal and then pushed the remote control.

There was a muffled explosion in the ambassador's office, and I saw the commandant run from his office and enter the ambassador's office. I ran down to the office with everyone else and saw the ambassador on the floor with the right side of his head missing. I knew he was dead, so I left the building under cover of the ensuing chaos.

ESCAPE

The escape plan was that we would split up into two teams and make our way down the Via Dei Corridor. We would make our way to the Piazza Pia that would lead us to the bridge over the Tiber River (Time Tevere). Our contact in Italy would have a nondescript boat waiting under the bridge.

We would follow the river until we reached the Tyrrhenian Sea and then make our way out into the Mediterranean Sea. The English stated that they would pick us up as we exited the Tiber River and take us to a safe area until we could arrange for transportation back to the United States.

Everything went as planned until we reached the intersection of the Via Dei Corridor and Piazza Pia. As I reached that intersection, I felt a sharp pain, and then numbness started in my left hand where they had implanted the chip. The numbness traveled up my arm past my shoulder and then I lost consciousness.

I woke up in a prison cell at the Vatican. The guard who was in front of my cell saw that I was awake and immediately called for the commandant of the World Police Force. I had been working with the commandant for a couple of weeks, so I was very familiar with him.

He took me from the prison cell to his office. I was expecting to be interrogated and had mentally prepared myself for the torture sessions that I knew were coming. He very politely asked me to sit down and seemed almost friendly. He was grinning like a Cheshire cat, and I knew that he was getting great enjoyment out of my predicament.

He said, "I have someone I want you to meet."

The door opened, and in walked the Ambassador of World Peace. He was alive, and with the exception of some scars, he seemed none the worse.

I was completely caught off guard because I knew he was dead. I saw him with half his head blown off. There was no way that this could be the same man. There had to have been a lookalike that fooled us. I knew that many world leaders always had a group of lookalikes who traveled with them, but I knew the ambassador, and I knew we killed the right person.

My mind was considering every possibility, and I could not figure this one out.

The commandant told me that indeed we did wound the real ambassador, and in fact everyone acknowledged that he was dead.

They had laid his body in a glass-enclosed coffin which was placed in the viewing room at the Vatican. They placed a cloth over his head because of the devastating wound, but the rest of his body, dressed in his favorite suit, was visible.

He had been lying in state for three days, and thousands of visitors had passed by in the viewing line when suddenly the guards noticed his right-hand start twitching. His fingers started moving, and then his entire hand and arm started moving. He reached up and removed the head cloth.

To everyone's surprise and amazement, his head was restored, and he was alive. He had some scars, but no visible injuries. He sat up, the guards removed the glass enclosure, and he got out of the coffin.

Everyone who was present in that viewing room started falling to the ground with their heads bowed toward the ground, proclaiming that he was a god.

The ambassador simply nodded his head toward the crowd and walked back toward his office, followed by a shouting crowd. The masses gathered at the Vatican, and whenever the ambassador would leave the office, the crowds would gather around him and shower him with praises.

The commandant stated that I had been unconscious for over a week, so they were just waiting for me to recover from the drugs that had been administered to me.

I asked, "How did you administer the drugs?"

The commandant stated, "The chip you had implanted had capabilities that you were totally unaware of.

"For two years, ever since your government started implanting the chips, we included two vials of very potent drugs hidden in the chip. The first vial would render you unconscious, and the second vial would kill you immediately."

He said, "Remember how in the United States when you locked yourself outside your car you could call the company, and they would push a button? When they pushed the button the doors of your car would automatically unlock.

"We included the same technology in the chip, but when we push a button, the chip releases one of the two drugs. One would incapacitate you, and the other drug would instantly kill you.

"We knew where you were, so we simply pushed the button that released the drugs in your chip, and you were instantly rendered unconscious.

"By the way, we also have terminated all of your comrades and the leaders of England, Italy, and Germany for their part in this treasonous act. I spared you instant death because of our relationship, and I wanted you to see how futile your actions have been. No one can defeat the Ambassador of World Peace."

The commandant further explained, "We have been able to track you and all of your comrades because of the embedded chip and the technology of the United States. We borrowed the technology from NSA that they used to compile databases of information on cell-phone usage. We expanded that technology so that we could track the movements of everyone in the world with an embedded chip. Citizens of the United States were unaware of your government's capabilities, but we knew when you met with the leaders of England, Germany, and Italy. We had been monitoring them ever since the ambassador had the confrontation with the EUC.

"The chip-tracking system has the built-in capabilities of sending an alert to the World Police Force whenever someone changes their pattern. When we noticed a change in patterns, we started looking at the records to see their past travels and who they met with. When the system sent an alert on the world leaders meeting with your president, we started monitoring their travels and the travels of everyone who crossed paths with them.

"We were aware when these three leaders met with the president of the United States, and knew something was amiss when they met with your team.

"We knew when you met in the Alps, and we have monitored you every step since then.

"We did not know what the plot was, and we were totally caught by surprise when the phone blew up and killed the ambassador.

"We eliminated your entire team, and tomorrow you will be sent to the prison that was built in the old

Roman Coliseum. You will be publically executed for this crime."

With that last statement, he waved his hand, dismissing me. Two guards entered the room, placed me in shackles, and transported me to a jail cell in the newly restored Roman Coliseum.

CHAPTER SIXTEEN
MOSES AND ELIJAH

I have just taken you through all of the events of my life that brought me to this prison. This morning I watched Andre and Brigette bravely walk out of this cell and peacefully go to their executions, singing of their faith in God.

I heard the thud of the guillotine as it ended both of their lives.

I will never forget the looks on their faces as the guards led them from this prison cell. I cannot get the image out of my mind of both of them bravely looking back at us in this cell and saying, "It is time for us to go home."

I rarely have ever witnessed such courage in two people who were not soldiers.

I knew early this morning I would also take that walk.

Tomorrow my life on this earth will be ended, and I don't care. I have lived a full life, and I have always tried to do the right thing. I know that I have made some mistakes, but none of that was intentional. I did the best I could with what I had.

I was thinking of my life's motto that I adopted in Mexico: *vivir come se puede y morir como se debe*. I will die as I should, and I will die with my pride intact. I have kept my vows to the end, and I have never compromised my beliefs.

It is almost midnight, and most of the people in this cell are sleeping. I have dozed at times, but mostof the time I am just thinking.

I suddenly became aware of the presences of two men standing right beside me. I did not see them approach, and I don't remember ever seeing them in this cell before. They are two men, and they look totally out of place in this cell.

One of the men is of average height, but his clothing and personification are unusual. He is wearing a sheepskin cape and a leather belt around his waist, and he is extremely hairy. His hair is very long, his beard extends almost halfway to his waist, and he looks like he is from another era.

The other man is slightly taller. He also has a beard and long hair, but it is neatly trimmed. He is wearing a long garment with a rope belt around his waist. He looks very dignified and almost kingly.

Both of these men kneel beside me, and the hairy one said to me, "Don't fear tomorrow. We are here to reveal some truth to you."

I asked, "Who are you?"

The hairy one said, "We are two witnesses who have come bearing witness to the truth."

I looked around the cell and made the following observation, "The jailors referred to these in my jail cell as the 144,000 witnesses, and now you two."

I said to the hairy one, "What's your name?"

He simply replied, "Elijah."

I asked, "Why have you come to me?"

Elijah answered, "We want to share some truth with you tonight so that you will understand what is happening and what you have been involved in."

I had to admit I was very interested. I wanted to know about the Ambassador of World Peace. I knew we killed him, and yet he came back to life three days later.

I looked at Elijah and asked, "Could we start with the Ambassador of World Peace?"

Elijah looked at me and answered, "You call him the Ambassador of World Peace, but the Bible refers to him as the Antichrist. The Bible says in the book of Revelation that he will suffer a mortal head wound and yet will live.

"You gave him that mortal head wound, yet he was intended to live for three and a half years more, so he had to come to life again and fulfill the biblical plan."

I then asked him, "What about my wife?"

The man who identified himself as Moses said, "We are in a period referred to in the Bible as the Seven Years of Tribulation."

Moses then asked me a question: "Would you have wanted your wife to endure what you have endured these three and a half years since Russia attacked Israel?"

I said, "No."

Moses then said to me, "God didn't want her to suffer this which has come upon the world either, so he sent his son, Jesus, to escort her from earth to her heavenly home. She is in heaven right now waiting for you."

I asked both of them, "Do you know what I have done in my lifetime?"

Moses looked at me and solemnly says, "If you remember your early childhood Bible school stories, I have also committed murder. I was forgiven."

I asked, "What must I do to be saved?" I remembered the terminology from the many conversations I had with my wife after I retired from Special Forces.

Moses smiled at me and said, "Believe in the Lord Jesus Christ, and you will be saved."

247

The remainder of that night, both Elijah and Moses stayed with me and were explaining the scriptures, starting with the book of Genesis, and early this morning we ended up the book of Revelation.

As they were finishing talking about the book of Revelation, the jailer who I despised called my name, and it was like he never saw the two men I was talking to. I stood up, took the shank I was holding in my hand, and started walking to the cell door. I had promised myself I would kill him before they executed me.

He had taunted so many innocent people who did not deserve the treatment he gave them. He was extremely sadistic and took great pleasure in mocking these innocent men and women. He was the worst bully I had ever met, and the world would be a better place without him.

I looked at him and thought, "You are such an easy target. I will drive this shank into your neck, even if it is the final thing I do."

There were three men waiting at the cell door to escort me to the arena for my execution. The one in the lead was the sadistic guard. Killing this guard was going to be so easy. The shank would enter his neck at the carotid artery and puncture the vein, and he would quickly bleed to death before help could get to him. He would have time to know I killed him, but no one would have time to save him.

NOW IS THE TIME

As I reach the jail cell door, I turned to the other prisoners and quietly said, "It is time for me to go home!"

I exited the door and lunged at the sadistic guard who I intended on killing. He froze in fear as I took the shank that was in my right hand and quicker than lighting jam it toward his neck.

I stopped just short of his neck, smiled, and dropped the shank on the floor in front of him. Then I turned, slowly walked down the hall, and stepped out into the arena. I looked back at the sadistic guard. He was still standing in the same spot, shaking violently, and it was obvious to all who saw him that he had soiled himself.

As I walked to the guillotine, I looked up toward heaven and said, "Honey, I'm almost home."

THE END

Made in the USA
Charleston, SC
06 February 2017